WALK HAND IN HAND INTO EXTINCTION

STORIES INSPIRED BY
TRUE DETECTIVE

EDITED BY
CHRISTOPH PAUL
AND
LEZA CANTORAL

WALK HAND IN HAND INTO EXTINCTION
Stories Inspired by True Detective

Edited By
Christoph Paul & Leza Cantoral

First Edition ISBN-13: 978-1-944866-00-6

Edited by Christoph Paul and Leza Cantoral
Cover Art by Mallory Rock
Interior Design by Joel Amat Güell

INDEX

I

A wise man once said the world needs bad men. You'd say I was a bad man, and you'd be right. I'd never claim otherwise, because I know we're necessary: we keep the other bad men from the door.

Bad men like Willis Wilkes. Bastard carried a shield, but had a liking for little kids, and I don't mean in an "Aw, shucks, ain't they so cute," sense. He took kids he knew wouldn't be missed and he used them up, before burying what's left like garbage.

Of course, in the grand scheme of things, what the hell does it matter? One more pervert? A few less kids? The world keeps turning and the Universe doesn't notice, doesn't care. Only we do. That's the supreme irony of life:

people care about things that don't really matter. Whatever they do, however much they struggle, things still end just the same.

Another wise man said that the world is indeed comic, but the joke is upon mankind. He was, I think, speaking about consciousness and its bastard daughters, conscience and guilt. Do you think a cockroach worries about the morality of eating your cereal? Do you imagine germs are even aware they make you ill? Only humans worry about meaning and morals or agonise about the ethics of taking antibiotics and the consequences of too many. If we were cockroaches, people like Willis Wilkes could do whatever they wanted and it wouldn't matter. We'd all be free, if freedom without knowing you're free is worth a damn. If anything is.

But, we aren't free and it does matter in some pathetic, finite way as we struggle to avoid the truth that it doesn't. Which was the reason why I had him pinned to the floor of his hallway as I stabbed at his face with a corkscrew.

A corkscrew is the perfect murder weapon: nobody ever got arrested for carrying one with intent to open a bottle, but they can puncture flesh with enough force and pop eyes as easily as they pop corks. Easier.

Wilkes was screaming as I stabbed him, begging

for mercy, but all I could think was how his blood seemed to run in spirals before it merged to cover his face in dark gore. The ragged-edged pin pricks where the corkscrew had gone in reminded me of stars in the night sky, only dark. Black stars. Sometimes, I look up at the sky and watch the stars. It's like a war's being waged in Heaven between light and darkness. Often, I wonder which is winning. Sometimes, I worry that, one day, I'll look up and see that all those stars have been snuffed out, leaving only dark stars burning cold and black. Like the holes I was putting in his face.

At last, my arm was beginning to weaken, aching from the repetitive blows. I drove the corkscrew into his neck – I knew
the spot – and blood began to pour out.

He shuddered and died. The light went out of his eyes. Extinguished, just like the dark stars...

He was dead. I stood up. It was over. Willis Wilkes would never hurt anyone again. I would, but only bad men; only people who deserved it.

I looked around. We were in his house. A dump. A hovel just outside the city limits. Quiet. Lonely. Hardly any furniture. The only signs of modernity were the home cinema and the laptop. A means for him to relive his obsession again and again. Yet, the images were never enough. Never.

On the walls, crude sketches of children, each, I was certain, identifiable as a child he had killed. He had arranged them in a pattern swirling out from a taller, central figure. Wilkes? Possibly. Where the children were drawn using red and black felt tips, the central figure was drawn mostly in yellow.

Of course, now I know the truth.

I set the house on fire. Cleansing flame. For once, light won out over the darkness. The good people of the city could go on living out their delusion that the world is anything but a meaningless wasteland full of horror.

My cell bleeped as I drove back into the city. It was a message from Jardin. My former partner. Now, Internal Affairs. A slimy bastard. I was glad to be rid of him and didn't relish meeting up with him. Putting him in IA had to be somebody's idea of a joke, or the purest evidence of the perverse meaningless of existence.

Jardin wanted to meet me in Castaigne's.

I considered ignoring him. Or, maybe messaging him back to tell him where he could go. But, instead, I let him know I'd be there. I don't know why. Does it really matter?

I drove over to the bar. Part of the glass frontage was boarded up, the rest was grimed over. The name flickered in yellow neon above the door.

Castaigne's is in the old part of town, where the gentry long ago gave way to the poor, the underclass, the scum of humanity. The bar would once have been more upmarket, but it had followed the district's slide into oblivion. Now, the only rich folk you'd find in it were slumming it, looking to score drugs or hookers. It didn't surprise me that half the dirty cops in the city, Wilkes included, frequented it.

Was Jardin's choice of venue a reflection of his own crookedness or habit from looking into its PD habitués? And, if the latter, did that say something about how he perceived me? Maybe I should've thought more about that.

I went inside. Jardin wasn't there.

I headed over to the bar. Asked for a whisky. That's all they seemed to serve, apart from bottles of something green and French.

I sat down in a corner booth. It was the perfect place to observe the rest of the bar without easily being overheard once Jardin arrived.

The bar was almost empty. A handful of

customers, each of them as rundown and dirty-seeming as the bar itself. None of them seemed to be cops. The interior decoration of Castaigne's was a sort of beige and washed-out yellow with the occasional blackish or greenish stain of mould and damp; it's a wonder the health officer hadn't closed it down.

I turned my attention from my depressing surroundings to the tabletop. Somebody had dragged a cloth across the sticky surface in a desultory attempt at cleaning it, producing swirls, which I studied, fascinated. The random shapes seemed almost to contain some indiscernible meaning. Then, it struck me: the swirl reminded me of the figures Wilkes had drawn on the walls of his house.

I found myself considering that image: I'd assumed it was analogous to a trophy, a record of every child he'd killed, or perhaps to the videos he kept as a reminder, a means to relive every murder. But, it seemed to be more than that; ritualistic. Like the swirls on the tabletop, it seemed to promise more meaning than I could discern. Somehow, I just knew that the meaning I sought revolved, like the children, around the central figure. If there was any meaning and I wasn't just imputing something to nothing.

I'd assumed the yellow-drawn figure was Wilkes,

standing at the centre of his victims, receiving their terrified adulation. But, what if it wasn't? To whom was he offering the children's lives?

No matter how I chased the thoughts about, I could never quite pin them down. Like the swirls, I seemed to be going around in circles, fixed upon the figure.

Then: "You came." The voice startled me out of my reverie. It was Jardin. I should have smelt him coming. Jardin's one of those officers who craft the image of the fat, sweaty detective who's eaten far too many donuts and spent more time at his desk than doing his job.

He shuffled his enormous backside onto the bench opposite me and his belly rocked the table. Having settled himself, Jardin pulled out one of those awful, huge red handkerchiefs with white spots and used it to wipe his face. The weather was warm, but not hot enough to justify the sweat that ran down his jowls from his bald pate. He was practically a cartoon.

"I said I'd be here," I told him. "What'd you want?"

He played nervously with his glass of whisky, then downed it in one go, before gesturing for the barman to bring him another.

"Well, what is it?" I asked him. "If you're planning to come out and declare your love for me, I have to tell you now, I don't go for fat, balding men with BO who work for Internal Affairs."

Jardin sputtered. He'd always been touchy about his sexuality. He liked to project the image of an avuncular ladies' man, but I'd seen the magazines he kept in his desk drawer, back in the day.

"I find your sense of humour distasteful," he said.

"I haven't changed."

"No, you haven't."

The conversation went on much like that for a while, with us catching up in a manner that did little to conceal out mutual dislike.

"Look," Jardin said at last, "some of the guys are beginning to lose patience with you. You're a loose cannon."

"Boom," I said, making him glare.
"You tread on toes; you poke your nose in where it's not wanted –"

"I even looked the gift-horse in the mouth, once," I said. "Come on, do you have to talk in clichés?"

"You've ruffled feathers."

"Oh, apparently, you do. Look, I get it, some of the guys are unhappy with me. Why? 'Cos I get results?"

"No, because you rock the boat."

It was then I told him that if he didn't stop talking

like that, I'd break his jaw.

The barman brought over his whisky and Jardin downed it in one and asked for another. I was still nursing my first.

"Look, just say whatever it is you have to say," I said.

"There's a natural order to this city and you're destabilising it. You're arresting the wrong people. Protected people. You're upsetting folk. Creating problems." He paused and took out his handkerchief and wiped his face again. I had to fight the urge to grab it and ram it down his throat. "They want me to bring you in on it, seeing as we're old pals."

"Bring me in on it?"

"Make you part of the brotherhood, the elite. They want you in the tent..." He trailed off when he realised I was glaring at him. "Well, you know the saying."

"There's another one about being able to see the stars because the tent's gone missing."

That just confused him. He frowned, then blinked as if dismissing my words and just went on: "They think you could fit right in. They know about your tastes."

"My tastes?" I asked. I had no idea what he was on about. "Are you fried chicken aficionados?"

"I'm talking about Crystal."

What can I say? Crystal was a stripper. I like strippers. A guy's got to blow off steam, right? Well, we got friendly. Then, somebody – the odds were he was sitting opposite me right then – dropped me in it and a posse of vice cops bundled into my apartment, expecting to find her there. Turned out she was only fifteen, dancing on a fake ID. They'd planned to get me on statutory rape. But, they could never prove I'd done more than watch her and it quickly blew over and Jardin moved on to new positions.

"What about Crystal?" I asked him.

Jardin laughed nervously. Then, his cell rang. He answered it and said "Uh-huh" several times before hanging up.

"Detective Wilkes is dead," he said.

I told him I knew.

Jardin grabbed his handkerchief again, dabbed his brow, then held it over his mouth as if nauseous.

"You killed him," he said through the cloth.

I didn't admit as much, but I guess he knew me well enough to tell I had.

"Dammit, you've gone too far," he said, mouth still covered. "You can't kill cops and expect to get away with it."

People always say that when you've proved you can.

"Look," he continued, "it comes down to this, man: either you knuckle under and do as you're told – and, believe me when I say, it can be a sweet deal; you could have all the young pussy you want – or, they'll deal with you. Drop you into prison with inmates who'd just love to say 'hi' to one of us; maybe worse."

I chewed my lip, as if I were thinking it over. I called over to the barman to bring over the bottle and I topped our glasses up. That's when it all came together.

Jardin gulped his down in one go and I did likewise, before refilling our glasses again.

Jardin gulped that down too – the man had to be sweating whisky. He hadn't even put the glass down before I brought the bottle down on the florid dome of his head. It didn't break the glass, but the blow did cause his face to slam down into the table. His nose burst and blood seemed to run in swirls across the tabletop.

Jardin raised his head and looked at me with unfocused eyes.

I smacked the bottle into him again and, this time, it shattered. He slumped back. I rammed the broken bottle into his face, again and again. If anything, it was better than the corkscrew.

I admit I did it in a rage, but I'd expected to get away with it; Castaigne's was one of those places where there are no cameras and folk are surprisingly unobservant. What I hadn't bargained with was that one of those "Uh-huhs" Jardin had mumbled into his cell must have been confirmation that I was there. Half-a-dozen IA cops had entered the bar while I was whaling on the bastard with the bottle and were standing there like slack-jawed idiots, watching. They probably wouldn't have been able to pin Wilkes on me or anything else, but I'd just butchered Jardin right in front of them.

Why didn't I go for my gun? They had theirs out, ready. I wouldn't have lasted a second, and I knew killing me was just what they wanted. Jardin had threatened me with hell in jail, but, knowing I'd killed Wilkes, they had to wonder how much I knew, and how much Jardin had told me. Dead, I'd be no problem.

Alive, I can bring them down. And, as much as I'd appreciate an end to the farce that is life, I'd rather give them grief.

Of course, how long I'll live is another matter.

That's why I'm in here. In jail, I'm plausible. In here, I'm a lunatic and nothing I say has any more value than the guy next door who swears he's Jesus and the President is a lizard in a man-suit.

But, even in here, I can still talk.

They're all in it together, all those dirty cops, and they have Internal Affairs tied deep into their nasty little conspiracy. They think they can do what they want. But, they never reckoned with me.

Especially now I've worked out who the figure was at the centre of Wilkes' wall art. It was on the whisky bottle, you see. There was a figure on the label, sort of like a monk in yellow robes. It looked quite like the figure he had drawn. It was a Yellow King Whisky, or something like that, I realised.

You see, it's not a who, but a what. That figure wasn't Wilkes or anyone human, it was a… map? It all goes back to Castaigne's. That's where they congregate. I'd be willing to bet that's where it all happens. The entire conspiracy revolves about Castaigne's.

Oh, roll your eyes if you like, imagine me mad, but you won't hold me forever. One day, I'll bring the entire rotten charade to an end.

But, what if the Yellow King is a who, after all, or maybe a what? The conspiracy given identity? Perhaps he is real. After all, a symbol has as much meaning as anything else: no meaning whatsoever. Imagine that he is: he might be an even bigger bad than any of us…

Maybe the truth is bigger than any of us can

comprehend?

Still, as I said earlier, none of this really matters. But, if it weren't for bad men like me looking out for people like you, I guarantee you'd imagine it did...

You might think I'm a prisoner here, but none of us are free. I'm just more aware of the truth than you. Perhaps, in some sense, I'm more free than you.

Sleep tight and we'll talk it over again tomorrow...

II

I'm sitting in a red El Camino outside of the liquor store by my mother's old place, and I can't help but think that this is all so cliché. There's a cigarette in my mouth, half-lit. *Cliché*. Bottle of whiskey beside me. *Cliché*. The only thing I'm lacking is a middle-aged partner with marital problems.

I look up at my reflection in the rear-view mirror and say, "You are a walking caricature, Clay." I stare at myself, blank faced, and then kill the end of my cigarette using the car's ashtray. *James Ellroy couldn't have written a more standard gumshoe*, I think to myself.

Hall & Oates are on the radio. "Maneater." Such a terrible song. But it's catchy, so I leave it playing.

Seems comical… listening to "Maneater" while my partner Darrell arrests this tall, Asian broad in hooker heels a block away. From what I can tell, he's giving her the typical *'I am the law'* spiel. He does it with every streetwalker. Thinks the exhibition of power turns'em on.

I can hear her howling at him. Saying *something*. The closer she gets, the clearer the words become. As she drags her heels toward the car, the woman yells, "Wrong lady. Wrong lady."

The police scanner screeches. It startles me, just a little.

I look to my right and Darrell has already positioned the woman against the side of the vehicle. "You know ya rights," he says, and opens the door to the backseat. There are already cuffs on her.

"No, no, no," I say. "I don't want her in my—" The woman ducks her head into the vehicle. Darrell shuts the door.

I curl my head to the side, toward her. The woman's perfume is overpowering. Bright red lipstick is smeared over two flaky slivers of flesh she calls lips. "What's your name?" I say to her.

"Let me go," she screams, kicking her four-inch heels into my seat.

"Is that Vietnamese or…?"

Darrell opens the door. I move the brown bag containing my whiskey. He slides into the passenger's seat.

"What do you got on her?" I say.

He shows me a small bag of heroin.

"Oh, for christsake, we're gonna drive all the way across town over a sugar packet?" I say.

"As opposed to what?" Darrell says, his arms folded. "Watching you chain smoke ya self to death in this smelly ass car? I'd rather go to—"

The speakers on the police scanner explode with static. Then, a voice chimes in, "...*Hardy and Haenick report to 86 Washington Boulevard, Bankston ... Caucasian male ... reportedly armed with a kitchen knife...*"—static.

I remove the bottle of Johnnie Walker from my bag and grin. I say, "How about we polish this off, let the whore go, and disarm a probable schizophrenic?"

Darrell doesn't look pleased. But he says, "Yeah, fine," and opens the car door. He steps outside and releases the woman from the backseat. She walks four feet before realizing she's still in cuffs, and then tails back.

"Idiot," he says, unlocking her. The prostitute stumbles away. Darrell gets back in the car. We drive off.

Washington Boulevard is not what you'd consider a *nice* place. It's been overrun with dealers and johns since the late-1970s. Ever since they integrated the block into the mayor's low-income housing plan, it's been a fucking mess. There's always talk now and again about reinvigorating the area, but nothing ever happens.

"I don't see nothin'," Darrell says, staring out of the passenger's seat window. We're both eying a block that's often referred to as The Pink Light District. A name earned for its recent influx of young male prostitutes. They sell their asses, mouths, and just about anything else Boston's suburban, white businessmen will buy.

"We're not even there yet," I tell Darrell, rounding the corner of Washington. He sighs. We're still a couple of minutes away our destination: the dark part of town.

The Pink Light District is flashy. Full of fags, some junked up—some not. They're all out carousing the block after 10:00pm. Looking for fun, looking for customers. The convenience stores will even stay open late, just for them. They know where their business comes from.

As we venture along Washington Boulevard, lights start to dissipate. The glitz fades away. We find ourselves in the middle of an abyss that is pure black, pure midnight.

At night, the city resembles a halfmoon cookie. Nobody wanders around these parts unless they're looking for, or hiding from, trouble. And I hate getting called out here. *Hate.* Nothing but crazies and kid touchers...

Mötley Crüe is on the radio now, and I can see that Darrell hates hearing their music as much as I do. His upper lip curls with disgust every time Vince Neil's voice chimes in through the speakers. "Turn this shit off," Darrell says. And I do.

"Keep your eyes peeled to the right," I say, and watch my left. For almost an entire block I can't see shit. Only abandoned homes and crack houses. "He's supposed to be 'round here."

In the distance, there's a figure—a man wobbling on the sidewalk. "Over here," I say to Darrell. The way that he walks makes him look like he's tripping over his own feet. There's something wrong with him.

My instinctive thought is that he's injured. Or has some kind of disability, like Cerebral Palsy. I picture my nephew, his unsteady hands failing to tie his own shoes. But as we roll in closer, I can see clear as day that that is not the case.

"Jesus," I say, but the word is near inaudible. My mind is aghast, and I almost drive past'em, lost in a fog of bewilderment. Darrell turns in my direction. Out of the corner of my eye I can see that he, too, is stunned by the sight to behold.

The man's face, pale and moist, is caked with blood. Some of it is still running. It all seems to be pouring out of two black sockets where eyes should be. And like the CB suggested, there is a knife in his hand—a kitchen knife. And that, too, is stained with blood.

My stomach goes cold. The kind of cold you feel when you get a certain kind of phone call in the middle of the night. Or come home to see your front door cracked just *slightly* open.

I swallow a wad of bitter spit lingering at the back of my throat and begin feeling around for my whiskey. My hand does not meet the bottle, but my foot does the brake.

"I don't know what the fuck to make of this one," Darrell whispers. "D'you think he did that to himself or…"

"*Billllly…*" the man screams. His voice is light, like a child's.

"How do you want to do this?"

"You kidding?" Darrell says. His eyebrows are arched, like the light-up McDonalds sign on 7th Avenue. "I want to take off in the opposite direction and tell the others we couldn't find this fucker. That's how I want to do this."

"What, you only play tough guy for the ladies? He's blind." I say.

"Here's what we'll do… You come up from behind, pull the knife away, and I'll get'em on the ground and cuff'em. It'll take a minute at most."

Darrell sighs. He knows it has to be done. Protect and serve isn't a preference, it's a credo.

He opens the car door and mumbles, "Why the fuck do I gotta do all the heavy lifting…"

I get out of the car. My first thought is to reach for my badge… but it's irrelevant here. So I go for my gun, instead.

The perpetrator is less than twenty feet away from me. He's heading toward an old, wooden building. There's a sign in its front yard that reads 'Free Flu Shots.' Darrell has already removed his leather Dockers and begun pacing behind him, silent in the night.

The man is oblivious to his surroundings. His head bounces back and forth as he stumbles forward. The knife dangles limp in his grasp. Small steps, one foot in front of the other—that's all he's got in'em.

Darrell, less than four feet away from our perp, gives me a nervous wink to let me know that he's ready. Each of his arms are outstretched, like he's prepared to give the guy a bear hug. A pistol glimmers from his waistline.

The entire time I'm thinking, *Hall & Oates.*

I cock Darrell a thumbs up. That's when he charges at the man, like he's Andre Tippet. Two-hundred and ten some-odd pounds of fat and muscle collide with the perp's buck-ten of bones. In an instant they both go tumbling to the concrete. The tip of the knife bends into the sidewalk. It slips out of the man's palm, but not before cutting him. He wails from the pain. The sound makes me take an initial step back. But then I find my balls and carry on to the sidewalk, where Darrell is lying atop the perp. His knee is pressed into the small of the man's back.

"Come on, slap the cuffs on'em," Darrell says. He sounds agitated. Scared.

I put my gun in its holster. Then I remove the handcuffs from my waist. "Easy, fella," I say to the man, who is writhing and twitching like he has Tourette's.

"*Billlllly*," he growls.

"Yeah, yeah, I'm sure you'll see Billy soon," I say, as I lock his dirty, blood stained wrists together. Darrell and I lift him to his feet. "What's your name?"

"*Billlllly*," the perpetrator says.

"That your name?" I say.

He grumbles something that sounds like a dismissal, and tries to drop to the ground. We catch him, though.

"The fuck's your deal, man?" Darrell says. We're carrying him over to my El Camino. All I can think about is how difficult it'll be to wipe away the stains from the interior.

"*Billlllllllllly*," the perp says.

"I don't think we're gonna get anything out of him," I say, and open the door to the backseat. I give the perpetrator a hard nudge into the vehicle. He seems unfazed, still lost in his own little world.

Darrell closes the back and we walk around to our respective doors. I get in and shut mine. Darrell does the same. The keys are back in ignition. Radio flickers on. This time it's Duran Duran playing. And I fucking *hate* Duran Duran. So I swap the station over to KROQ 106.7, and we're back to Hall & Oates. This time it's "Kiss On My List". It's an OK song. Not my favorite, but I can tolerate it enough to drive this gory-eyed fuck to the emergency room.

Darrell picks up the CB and says, "En route to Bankston General Hospital with the perp. He's bleeding out pretty bad, needs immediate medical attention." But the report doesn't go through the receiver. The machine is not lit up. Typically there is at least two glowing red lights that let me know it's working, but they're blackened.

"The fucking thing is off," I say, and reach for the switch. But it's turned on. The scanner is dead.

"Well, Clay, that's just lovely," Darrell says. "Let me g—"

"*Fee! Fie! Foe! Fum! I smell the blood of a royal cunt,*" the perp says. I look at him through the rear-view mirror. He's grinning. Facing forward—in Darrell's direction—and *smiling.*

Darrell sets the CB down. He looks back to the perp, a tired expression on his face, and says, "How would you like to lose your tongue, too?"

"I can *smell* you," the perp says.

"I can change that," Darrell says, and belts him across the nose with his right fist. I almost flinch from the quickness of the motion, but I'm used to that from Darrell. The perp's head bounces against the side of the window and for a second I fear it'll crack. The window, not his head.

"Easy now," I say to Darrell, who returns his hand to his side. "I don't want to do any extra clean up."

The perp slides back to the center of his seat. There is no longer a smile on his face. His lips are curled downward into, not quite a frown, but something similar—and more dramatic. "*Billllly,*" he wails, his throat raspy. Blood dribbles from his mouth, and then sprays from his nose in a sneeze.

"You called it, Clay. The guy's a skitzo," Darrell says, and shakes his head. "Just another lunatic…"

"*Billy, your father's looking for you,*" the perp says, and then my stomach drops. I start to think, *what the fuck is this creep up to? What has he done?*

"Who is Billy?" I say, again; this time sterner.

"Don't indulge him," Darrell says, and lights up a cigarette. "The last thing I want to do is spend my Saturday night listenin' to you to carry on a conversation with this fuckwit about his imaginary friend."

I poke Darrell with my elbow, and he almost drops his cigarette. "Who the fuck is Billy?" I say to the perp.

The perp lowers his head—toward me—and flashes a bright, blood stained smile. "*You ever been to Calgary, Clay?*" he asks me, his voice sounding like gravel skidding against concrete. The free-range use of words almost jolts me. But not as much as the way he says my name, or the question itself…

I have been to Calgary. It's where my wife was born. *Ex-wife.* But I tell'em, "No," and he doesn't look satisfied with the answer.

His bizarre, almost-frown returns to his face and he begins howling once more, "*Billllllllly,*" as if it pains him to say it.

"I answered your question," I say, "Now you answer mine; why do you keep saying that name?"

"*Billlllly*…." the perp says.

"Ya know, it feels like a Taco Bell sorta night," Darrell says. "How 'bout we go through the drive-thru?" He turns his head to the perp. "You like the soft taco supreme?"

"*I want to put a knife in your throat*," the perp says.

Darrell's eyes widen.

"I don't think you know who you're talking to. My partner here is a decorated war veteran," I lie, looking in my rear-view mirror. "Killed thirteen guys in the 'Nam. Two with his bare hands. If he wanted to, he could—"

"*Billlllly*," the perpetrator whines, cutting me off. "*Billlllllllllly… Billy, say hello to the nice men…*" He thrusts his body sideways, spinning his back toward us. There's a hand between both of his. It's small and slathered with blood. He flings it to the dashboard. It bounces off of the radio and lands in my lap. A *child's* hand lands in my lap.

I slam my foot on the brake. Something in my head parts ways with any foundation of reason, or logic. I've been trained to remain level-headed in situations like this. Trained to keep control. But I'm old. And there are not many years left in my career.

Fuck it.

I abandon what I'm taught. And I already know what Darrell's going to say… Even if the look of horror on his face from the child—*toddler's*—hand may be enough to let me know he'll forgive my actions.

I remove my gun, naturally, and swing my hand to the backseat.

Darrell, prepared for what's to come, winces. With my finger wrapped over the trigger, I pull the hammer back. The perp grins.

I fire. But nothing happens.

Both confusion and relief wash over me. I suddenly feel like a man who's killed someone in a dream and woken to a safe reality. "Jesus, Clay," Darrell says, his voice quiet and short of breath. He raises his hand to the top of my gun and lowers it with his palm. "What the fuck?" Darrell's eyes glance down to the hand in my lap, then back up at my face. "At least take'em outside first." He strips part of his jacket away from his stomach, revealing a pistol near his belt. "And take my gun, it never jams." From the holster to my left hand, his gun goes. I open my door.

"*Billllllllllllly*," the perp cries. Darrell yanks the backseat open. He grabs the perp by his dampened collar and pulls him out onto the street.

At this point I'm already having doubts about

ending this man's life. The anger is present, but the adrenaline is gone.

Do I really want to kill this guy?

The street is empty. It's dark. There doesn't seem to be signs of life for quite some distance.

"Over there," Darrell says, and points his finger at a broken fence between two boarded up houses. Using his right hand, Darrell shoves the perp to the ground. He lands on his knees. I put my gun away, but continue to hold Darrell's.

I walk over to the side of my car, the gun in hand, and I point it at the perp. "Who the fuck did you kill?" I say, my voice shaky—but not exactly lacking confidence.

The perp says nothing. He just stares at the ground.

I start thinking, *What if he hasn't killed anyone?* But then my mind rebuts, *what are the odds of that?*

"If you're gonna do it, you better make it quick," Darrell says, and starts dragging the man from the pavement to the dying, brown grass between both houses. I follow them, but my head is a clouded mess. I don't know what the fuck to do.

We reach the gap. Darrell drops the perp and backs away ten feet. The perp remains still. I aim the end of the barrel at the man's forehead. I know he knows what

I'm doing. I can feel it. It's in the air. But he does nothing. Not a single word is spoken between us.

Child murderer…

My finger locks around the trigger of the gun. I think for a moment, and then pull it.

As we walk back to the car, a sinking feeling develops in my guts. It's not the first time I've killed somebody. Won't be the last, either. But I feel as if what I did was wrong. Not for moral reasons, mind you—but something about it just feels *off*. Like I've left home with the stove on, or without my car keys. There's something I'm missing.

I open my car door. The bloodied childlike hand is resting on my seat. From here, I can see the thing in its entirety. At the end of it, there's a hole—like where a plug might fit. I reach for it.

It's cold. The hand is cold. And plastic.

36

III

Leonard Jakes pulled the label off his sweaty bottle of Coors and rolled the sticky piece of paper into a ball, flicking it into the sky. He let out a sigh and fished into his pocket for his crumpled packet of Bugler and Zig-Zags. He rolled a smoke and lit up. The old telephone line spools and folding chairs stuck out beside the parking lot were all that passed for a smoking section at the Breeze Inn. Leonard wanted to drink *and* smoke, so he sat outside.

The screen door clattered as the girl passed outside, a bag of trash in her hand.

"Hey Jessi," shouted Leonard, "when you get a chance, one more."

Jessi tossed the trash and walked over. "That's four, Leonard. I thought you quit drinking. You ain't ordered nothing but RC Cola for six months."

"Yeah." Leonard blew out a long trail of smoke. "Sometimes I quit. Sometimes I start back up again. Today I started." Leonard swallowed the last of the beer in his bottle. "I gotta go see Preacher."

Jessi's smile turned into a grimace. "Damn. I don't like that man. He comes in here once a week and gets real drunk. Talks to anybody. Crazy shit come outta his mouth. My momma don't like him none, tells me to stay away from him. I guess he was handsome enough, once, though."

Leonard shook his empty bottle and smiled. "You know, Sugar, I remember when we couldn't get Coors in Louisiana. People were crazy for it then because they couldn't get it. But it ain't that good. People always want what they can't – or shouldn't have. Now I know you young girls don't always listen to your mommas. But when it comes to Preacher, you better."

"I'll get you that last beer, Leonard." Jessi shook her head to herself. "What you going out there for, anyway?"

"Beaux up at the Piggly Wiggly called. Preacher asked for a grocery delivery. Pay extra, good tip. But none of Beaux's boys would go up, so he asked me. Got a case of canned shit in the trunk. Headed out cause I need the money."

"Huh. Well don't spend it all on beer." Jessi turned around and strutted back into the Breeze.

"Yeah," said Leonard, sitting alone.

The old Crown Vic bounced down the rutted road, dried hard in the summer heat. He had the directions written on a piece of Zig-Zag paper. He'd been out to the old church a couple of times; hard as hell to find. Leonard rotated the piece of paper and tried to read his own handwriting.

Leonard was flustered, a bit too drunk to drive, and distracted. He kept seeing the sight of Jessi's tight little ass bouncing from one side to the other in her cut-offs as she sauntered back into her momma's bar. Momma had been a hot piece of ass in her day as well, before too much Jim Beam and tobacco ruined her. Jessi didn't smoke and seemed to just drink lite beer and Diet Coke. She smelled fresh and sweet – clean. Something you didn't run across too much in Vermillion Parish. Leonard couldn't get the memory of her smell out of his nostrils, even bathed in the stink of Bugler. He kept seeing that vision of her walking away from him flash before his eyes.

"Stop thinking with your dick," he mumbled, pulling his car to the side of the empty road. He polished the sweat off his face with an old bandana. Leonard had to deal with Preacher and he needed to be clear headed. He had once been a man like Preacher – a creature of his appetites. Drink, drugs, women – even when the women didn't want it. But he'd gotten his life together. He'd found a program and he was straight. Sure, sometimes he'd fall off the wagon and land in a puddle of beer, but he didn't hurt girls any more. Just beer. Just a few beers. He had self-control.

Leonard pushed himself back into his seat as far as he could go and shoved the bandana down his pants. With his right hand he masturbated, relishing the memory of that clean smell and the sight of that tight, young ass. When he was done he wiped and tossed the bandana into the glove box. Then Leonard got out of the car, walked a few yards into the tall grass of the surrounding fields, and vomited up his gut full of beer. He had self-control. His head was clear. Leonard Jakes got back into his car and found Preacher.

The church stood out in the open. At one time it was probably surrounded by marsh and tall trees, covered in Spanish moss. But all that was gone – drained away for agriculture. Now even the crops had vanished to make room for oil and fracked gas. Mother Nature was creeping back in, but now she had an uglier, harsher face – a face of ruined beauty, torn up by too much hard living.

The ruins of the parsonage were unlivable, but the church itself was still serviceable. It was clear Preacher was living in there. A big black Dodge van with the words JESUS SAVES painted on the side was sitting in front of the building. Leonard pulled his Crown Vic in next to it, parking under the lone tree still left at the place.

He climbed out of his car and went around to the trunk, pulling out the box of groceries. The smell of gas exhaust and the hum of a generator filled the air. A swamp cooler hung roughly out of one of the church's windows. The swamp cooler's noise joined that of the generator to create a general cacophony, echoed by the cicadas in that lonely tree.

Leonard walked across the overgrown parking lot. He banged on the church's double doors - nobody answered. The doors were locked but there was no deadbolt, so by pushing gently Leonard was able to force the doors open and step inside. The smell of body odor and musty swamp cooler air hit Leonard full in the face. It was a wall of stink, layered with cooked food, unwashed dishes, and garbage.

"Guess Preacher's gone feral," Leonard mumbled

to himself. "PREACHER! HEY PREACHER!"

Leonard walked around the old church pews. He remembered that the place had once been used by a real congregation; a bunch of Pentecostals, whose organ and loud singing could be heard for miles around. Gone, now.

Preacher came to town about three years before, he said from New Orleans, and started holding "services" in the place. He said he had a lease from the family that owned it but nobody believed him. He seemed to be a crank who used a fake minister's collar to fuck young girls who ought to know better. Probably did drugs and got drunk every night. All the stuff Leonard had resolved to avoid on his program.

Leonard walked around the pulpit. To its right was a closed door with a sign that read "Church Office." The cross on the wall over the pulpit was gone and somebody had hung a sheet up there on the wall covering something up. Leonard rapped his knuckles on the church office door. There was movement inside.

"Hey Preacher," Leonard yelled again.

"Leonard Jakes, that you?" An Irish Channel accent barked from the back of the church. Leonard spun around and Preacher was standing in the open double doors.

"Yeah, Preacher, it's me. Up from Beaux at the

Piggly Wiggly. Got your groceries."

Preacher stepped inside the church and pulled the doors closed behind him. He wore a cheap black three piece suit, dusty and faded, and a black shirt with white clerical collar. On his head was an old black fedora he'd flattened in semblance of a parson's hat.

"Well come on in, Brother Jakes, and sit a spell." Preacher indicated a pew towards the middle of the church.

"Where should I put the groceries? You got a kitchen? Or the *office?*"

"No, no," said Preacher stepping forward. "Just drop the box on the altar and I'll take care of that later. What I owe you?"

"Thirty-three fiddy. Plus Beaux said something about a tip."

"We'll make it an even fifty. How about that?"

"Thanks, Preacher. That's mighty good of you. I think I'll take that seat."

Leonard pulled a wooden handled Bowie knife from his pants, tucked away at the small of his back, and gently laid it on the pew next to him. Preacher smiled nervously and sat down on the seat just in front, turning around to face Leonard. He pulled a long metal flask from his coat.

"Drink, Leonard? Smells like you had a few already."

"Nah, Preacher, I quit that stuff. I got on a program."

Preacher spun the lid off the flask and took a long pull. The smell of cheap bourbon filled the air. "What kinda program is that Leonard?"

"I met a man. A good man. About a year ago. He was into some Chinese or Japanese bullshit, but he talked a lot of sense about how to channel your mind, focus your thinking. Meditation, they call it. Helps you control your urges. There's monks over in the mountains in Asia that can go a month without eating, drinking, or pissing, Preacher, they've got so much self-control. Makes a man less…thirsty."

"Oh yeah?" Preacher took another pull. "I've heard of that. When I was in college. But I put that stuff behind me and embraced the word of our Lord, Jesus Christ. I'm a saved man. You think much about that stuff Leonard? Your salvation?"

Leonard snorted. "Yeah, I used to think about that stuff. But I figure I'm headed to hell already. Ain't most of us? So I'm just trying to walk a line while I'm alive on this earth. Jesus might'a saved you Preacher, but not from the bottle."

Preacher laughed, throwing back his head, revealing a row of white teeth. He was living rough out here, Leonard thought, but he was keeping clean.

"Everything in moderation, Leonard, even moderation."

Pride. Pride and vanity, Leonard thought. Here was a man with no self-control.

Leonard looked Preacher square in the eye. It made his heart race a little bit to hold such a firm gaze. "Preacher, let me ask you something. What have you got locked up back in that office?"

Preacher's smile fell and he looked over Leonard's shoulder toward the closed door. "Leonard, thanks for bringing up those groceries. Here's a hundred, how about that? Now, I've got to get back to cleaning up outside. I'm looking to re-open this place soon!"

"Preacher," Leonard held that gaze as hard as he could, leftover beer bile rising in his throat, "how 'bout you tell me what you've got locked up in that office?" He laid his hand on his knife.

Preacher stood up and held out his hands, as if he were about to begin a sermon. "Leonard, you know we don't know each other that well. We're not friends. I've seen you a few times at the Breeze, but now you're in my home, in my *church*. Let's show some manners, cher, eh?

Did you know that a long time ago, after I left Tulane, I worked for a carnival? The Rinaldi Brothers Traveling Show! I had one job: to stand in front of whatever attraction I was assigned to that day and talk people into coming in to see the freaks on the inside. It cost a dollar. Cheap. You'd think anybody'd drop a dollar, right? Nope. People had to be talked out of their money, one at a time. A dollar might as well be a hundred dollars or a thousand dollars, Leonard. It's damn near as easy to get one as the other. I got good at it! Look at this place! It's not so different, Leonard, except now I'm not showing people freaks, I'm helping them get better – to heal their wounds and save their souls. One at a time. Sometimes that's easy – sometimes it takes work. And this ministry needs money – it needs those dollars."

"So what are you saying, Preacher, you're out here carnival barking for Jesus? It looks like you don't need money that bad. You just gave me a hundred."

"I'm saying you and me never had a relationship before but I can see that we should start one. You're on that program of yours and I'd like to learn more about it. I surely would. But maybe I can help you, too. As I grow this ministry I'm going to need helpers. Maybe you keep on bringing up my groceries, once a week, and I keep paying you like I did today. See, I've got an *old dog* locked up in my office. Sick old thing. Been with me for years and he gets violent around strangers. You just remember that and when you go back to town you tell people that and at this same time every week you can deliver my groceries and get paid."

Leonard grunted and smiled down into his lap. "You're interested in my program, huh? That man I met – he's a bit like you. Educated. He reads a lot, got a lot of books. He spotted me out one night at the Breeze Inn, drunk, trying to grab under some young thing's skirt, and he asked me to step outside. He knocked me down. Harder than I've ever been knocked down before. Then he offered me his hand. He gave me work, odd jobs. An offer just like yours. But he taught me things, too, about how to meditate, how to control my urges. How to be *respectable* and channel my energy into something useful. Then, about six months ago, he had me at his house and he took me inside and showed me one of those books, Preacher. It was a play, but like nothing I ever read in school. There were words in there I didn't understand: Cassilda, Camilla, Hyades, *Carcosa*. It opened my mind, it changed my mind, and all of a sudden I felt different. And when I turned and looked at this man, in my eye, he looked like *a King*. Maybe you seen this man around, too?"

Preacher flopped back down in his pew. He let out

a sigh. "Ok, I was told somebody would be coming today for the merchandise, but I didn't expect you. I should have known. I thought *He* might come in person. Do you have the money?"

"I dunno, Preacher, is the merchandise unspoiled? I know about you and them girls, Preacher. I bet when you was on the carny circuit you got more than dollar bills out of some of your customers."

"I might do it to some, but not this one. I need the money. This one is 'bespoke' you might say. This ministry needs money to establish itself. Besides, there's plenty of cooch down at the Breeze to keep a man satisfied."

In a flash, Leonard picked up his Bowie knife and ran it across Preacher's throat. The fake minister's eyes widened and his mouth fell open as an ugly red gash opened, pouring blood down the front of his clothes. The man gurgled, trying to speak, but only tiny bubbles of blood came out of his mouth.

Leonard stood up and wiped his knife on Preacher's clothes. "It's too bad, sir - you were dead when I got here with the groceries. That's the story the sheriff's already been told. See, Preacher, we thought you were one of us, but you got no self-control. Eventually you were gonna take the wrong merchandise or talk to the wrong person – and *He* can't allow that. We can't have it. So good night – maybe we can talk again when we both get to where you're headed."

Leonard fished around in the dying man's pockets and pulled out a keyring. He sheathed his knife and strode back to the office. Moving fast he unlocked the door. A young girl was lying on the floor on her side. She couldn't have been more than 16. Raven black hair, olive skin, but with terrified blue eyes that looked up into Leonard's face.

"Aw, honey," said Leonard, "don't be scared. This'll be over soon. I'm gonna take you somewhere where you'll be treated real nice."

He bent over and picked up the girl and tossed her over his shoulder. She struggled and tried to talk through the rag in her mouth. He headed for the main door of the church, stopping to look down into the dying Preacher's face. His eyes fluttered, the life draining out of him.

Leonard spoke: "See Preacher, this is my program. When I looked into that book I got clarity, I knew what I needed to do. I help *Him* get what he needs and I get what *I* need. Self-control. Freedom from my desires. And safety for me and the ones I care about. See I do this for *Him* and he leaves the girls down at the Breeze alone; Jessi, her mom, and their friends. They never end up like *this*, tied up in your goddamned office waiting on a delivery boy to do a pickup. I'm taking care of my own with this,

Preacher. But you were never gonna join the program - I could see it in your eyes. You wanted the girl. Jessi. *My girl.* And someday, if I'm good, *He's* gonna give her to me. Not you. So you see, it was always gonna be like this between us."

Leonard Jakes stepped passed the dying man, just as his eyes flickered closed, carrying the struggling girl on his shoulders. He walked down the aisle of the church and into the muggy Louisiana afternoon. The memory of a sweet clean, innocent smell filled his nostrils.

IV

THE YELLER KING

DAVID W. BARBEE

"Stop telling me to kill people."

Justin's dog had been talking to him for years now. It was a shaggy yellow Labrador that his mother had named "Yeller" after the movie. Yeller was still a puppy when he began speaking to Justin, who quickly realized that he was the only one who could hear the baritone words coming out of the dog's snout. Justin kept it a secret, and like all secrets it became a heavy burden. The dog usually spoke of vengeance and blood and mighty reckonings, a great sea of nothingness floating the world in a leaky rowboat.

Yeller followed him out of the house and up to the street. "You're going for another walk," the dog said.

"What are you walking away from?"

"It's just a walk," Justin said. When the house was out of sight Justin took out his cigarettes and lit one. He was old enough to enjoy smoking but still young enough to want to hide it from his mother.

They came to the end of the street and crossed the intersecting road. On the other side was a thick forest, and Justin walked in with Yeller right behind. They wound their way through the pines, on no discernible path, moving deeper into the shadows of the woods.

Yeller trotted up to Justin's flank and stood below the hand holding the cigarette. "You hide this from your mother," he said. "She lives in a fantasy world."

"Yes," said Justin. "A fantasy world where the only difference from reality is that I don't smoke."

"And a dog talks to you."

"And a dog talks to me."

"It's enough," Yeller said. "There are no small deceptions. Each and every one is an aberration to reality, the tiniest crack in the façade. In enough time you will tell so many lies that the façade will disintegrate and your reality will merge with the truth."

Justin took a long drag off his cigarette. "Reality. Truth. And killing people."

Yeller wagged his tail. "Don't be confused. This

isn't a wheat and chafe argument. This world is all chafe."

"I think I've proven that I'm not listening to you."

"But you don't deny that I speak the truth."

"The truth is that a talking dog is going to follow me around forever. Or at least until you get hit by a car."

They ventured deeper into the forest. Justin picked his way through the trees and Yeller scouted all around him, never straying more than a few yards from his master. He sniffed through the fallen leaves and pissed on a few trees, muttering things that Justin couldn't hear. They stopped as Justin put out his cigarette on a stone, taking care to grind out every cinder.

Yeller trotted up with jagged leaves tangled in his shaggy golden hair. "Where are you going?" he said. "You're wandering further than usual."

The dog wanted him to argue, and Justin knew to be noncommittal. "I'm just wandering, I guess," he said.

"There are no random steps taken," Yeller said. "You are being summoned, drawn into the primal unknown to face your destiny."

Justin said nothing. He put the wrinkled cigarette butt in the pocket of his jeans and took out his pack to light up another. Then he walked away. Yeller watched him for a moment before running to catch up. They kept walking, the leaves crunching beneath their steps, Justin stealing glances back the way they came so he didn't get lost. He was leading them northeast, toward who knew what.

Yeller barked.

Justin looked to see the dog staring at something, his legs stiff and his nose pointing through the trees. He walked over, the cigarette drooping from his lips, taking his time. He figured this might be another one of Yeller's tricks. He stood over the dog and looked in the direction his snout was pointing.

"What you figure that is?" Yeller said.

"It's a cabin," Justin said, squinting at the big wooden box with saplings growing up against the walls. "Looks old."

Yeller looked up at him, waiting for direction.

"Let's check it out," Justin said.

"This is strange," Yeller growled.

"Still just walking, Yeller," he said as they approached the cabin. "It's not as ominous as you think." They stopped a few paces from the open door of the cabin, the interior black and shadowed.

"This place has been here a long time," Yeller said. "A hunting cabin, probably, but it's abandoned now. There's something inside, though. I smell blood." The dog looked up. "Will you go in?"

"Into the spooky abandoned cabin?" Justin said, and sucked hard on his cigarette. "Why not?" He walked up to the doorway and stubbed the cigarette out on the splintery doorframe, standing right in front of the dark interior of the cabin. A cold breeze seemed to pulse in and out of the doorway, breathing on Justin and lighting up the cinders that fell from his cigarette.

Yeller watched him disappear into the shadows. The dog slowly walked up and sniffed at the cigarette ashes scattered at the foot of the doorway. When he was sure there was no trace of smoke or burning, Yeller stepped inside after his master.

The cabin was a single room, with just a few rays of light from a dirty window in the back wall. The place was coated in dust and spider webs. Yeller saw Justin down on his haunches, squatting low and examining the floor. The dog came close to see, but his nose already knew what it was from the stench lingering in the air.

"Blood," Justin said, lighting up another cigarette.

From the flash of the lighter they could see the scene. A circle of blood covered the center of the floor, coating the wooden planks like dark mud. Justin raised the lighter and they saw the source of the blood sitting before them like a monument of mutilated flesh with a halo of flies buzzing over its head.

Yeller and Justin took their time studying the specifics of the dead man. He was the recipient of carefully applied violence, a terrible wrath that had been cultivated and controlled. He sat in a wooden chair, nude, a rope wound around his waist to hold him up with perfect posture. The hands rested on the arms of the chair, a nail through each palm to hold them fast. The feet looked to be nailed to the floor as well, caked in dried blood.

Between his legs was an open gash where most of the blood had spilled. The missing genitals were stuffed into his mouth, a bit of hairy meat parting his lips. The top of his face was hidden by his scalp, cut and peeled from his head and draped over his eyes like a mask. The skin was dry and shriveled, the blood turned to crust. The halo of flies took turns crawling around on his exposed skull.

"Is it ominous yet?" Yeller asked.

Justin blew a plume of smoke at the dead man.

"This is someone's work," the dog said. "This man was prepared, made into some psychopath's art project."

"Looks like he was tortured," said Justin. "The scalping and castrating didn't kill him, the loss of blood did."

"This is evil, Justin. This is horror born from hell. He couldn't have deserved such pain. He was some innocent man, going about his business, before some monster leapt out of the shadows and grabbed him, brought him back here. Now you see, Justin. This is the wickedness I'm always telling you about."

"You've been begging me to go to the grocery store and mow everybody down with a machine gun."

"I've never begged you, Justin."

Justin sucked on his cigarette. "This isn't just evil," he muttered. "It's somebody's ritual. This is somebody's murder den. But then why would he leave the body here to rot?"

"Part of his ritual, perhaps."

"Maybe," Justin said. "Maybe it's like you said, an art project. Maybe he wanted somebody to find it."

Yeller sniffed at the blood and took a step back before sitting on his haunches. "Justin," he said softly, "we found this for a reason. You were meant to be here, to find this room and the horror that's inside. It's up to you now, to bring it into the light, because the *creature* that did this? He has to be stopped. A thing like this can only lurk in the shadows for so long. You're looking into the eyes of evil, Justin, and you have the power to end it."

Justin chuckled, and in the quiet darkness it sounded vicious. "I told you to stop telling me to kill people."

"It's not like that!" Yeller snapped. "I'm just saying… take revenge. For this man and who knows how many others this has happened to. You can find this killer. I'll help you. You can become the hand of justice and rid the world of this evil."

"You just want me to kill."

"And this is the best reason to do it!" Yeller said. "Besides, this is all evidence and now that you've seen it you are a witness. Perhaps you are an accessory, if the police decide it. They could actually pin this murder on you if they find out about it. All the more reason to find the killer yourself and be done with it."

Justin looked over at his dog. "How would we find him?"

"I can track his scent!" Yeller said, his tail wagging.

"And the police would never have to know?"

"Precisely!"

Justin stood up, sucking hard on his cigarette. He walked around the circle of blood to the back of the cabin. The dog watched. Justin went to the dirty window, where dusty curtains hung on either side. Justin took out his lighter and held a flame to the bottom of each curtain. "The first thing to do," he said, "is destroy the evidence."

Yeller let out an excited bark.

The two of them left the cabin as the flames ate

away the curtains and spread to the old wood that made up the ceiling. The thatch roof began to smoke as Justin and Yeller walked back into the woods. The fire overtook the cabin as they left the woods and walked up the street back to Justin's house. Yeller's tail wagged the whole way.

Later that night they heard the sound of sirens and fire trucks. Yeller lay on the floor next to Justin's bed, wondering how much of the forest had burned along with the cabin. He listened to Justin lying in the bed above him. He knew he wasn't asleep, but his breathing was slow and shallow. The dog's tail stopped wagging and his mind drifted away, dreaming his evil dreams.

Yeller woke up suddenly in the middle of the night. He wasn't certain what was happening, but he knew Justin was betraying him.

Very quickly, Justin wrapped the dog in a sheet and tied it up with rope. The dog tried to buck his body and gnash his teeth at his master's hands, but within moments he was wrapped tight and thrown over Justin's shoulder. He carried him outside into the backyard and into the woods. He walked a few yards before he dropped the dog on the ground. Then Justin lit a lantern and set it next to Yeller. The dog's snout protruded from the cloth cocoon and one eye could see a shovel in the soft light leaning against a nearby tree.

Yeller's brown eyes went wide as he watched his master dig. "Justin?" he said. "What's happening?"

Justin silently plunged the spade into the dirt, repeating the motions again and again. Yeller watched him carve out a dog-sized hole in the forest floor.

"Why are you doing this?" the dog said.

Justin kept digging. Yeller sniffed and smelled smoke in the air from the burnt cabin. "You… you are the one, Justin. You killed that man in the cabin. Didn't you? After all these years you finally did it."

"No," Justin said. He stopped digging and turned to look at the dog, his face lit by the lantern's soft glow. "You're trying to confuse me." He started digging again.

"Then why?" Yeller barked.

"Because *you* killed that man in the cabin. You tortured him and displayed him, and you waited for me to find him so you could deliver your fancy speech about wickedness and the hand of justice. I've been thinking on this all night, waiting for you to go to sleep. You killed to get me to kill… to get what you always wanted."

The dog stared for a moment. "Oh… okay, look…"

Justin's shovel stabbed into the earth once more. "I figured you'd be happy," he said. "Happy that I'm finally killing someone. Even if it's you."

Yeller said nothing. His face lay flat on the ground, limp, motionless, one eye staring up at Justin as he finished digging the hole. Justin lay the shovel aside and came to pick up his dog. Yeller's head hung limp as he lifted him and laid him in the ground. He picked up the shovel and began filling the hole. The dog said nothing as he was buried alive. He just stared up at his master, and in the dim glow of the lantern the man stood tall in the darkness like an avenging angel.

walk hand in hand into extinction

V

A BRIEF HISTORY OF BAD MEN

Tom
Leins

We are on the fifth floor of the Intercontinental Hotel. The Cantonese whorehouse takes up the entire fourth floor of the building. I'm gaffer-taped to a wooden chair in a room that is small enough to be a prison cell. There is a rack full of shotguns above the TV and a long brown stain on the ceiling, roughly the size of a body. Gilligan referred to it as the 'Games Room'.

Gilligan is huge. He looks more like a wrestler than a cop. In truth, he's barely a cop. He's a small time racketeer with a badge and a gun. The sleeves of his hounds-tooth jacket are rolled up to the elbow. His hair is scraped back and hangs limply over his collar. He has the bloated features of a long-time vodka drinker. The puckered pink scar between his left eye and his jawbone pulses angrily. He hits me in the face – twice, in quick succession. I work a tooth loose with my tongue and spit it at his feet.

"I've always had a soft spot for you, Mr. Rey ... in the middle of Clennon fucking Valley."

The sickly voice belongs to a cadaverous sex offender known as Meat-Rack. He is wearing a dark suit and a short-brimmed hat. His clothing smells like a hooker's mattress. He's half Cantonese and all-the-way sick. He has links to the Triad, but he's not a major player.

He coughs in my face and it smells of Babycham.

"Mr. Gilligan, please prepare the crate."

Two days earlier.

"I'm sorry – I've interrupted your lunch, haven't I?"

The woman in the trench-coat looks nervous. She has sleepy-looking brown eyes and her hair is a soft shade of honey-blonde.

I crumple my beer can and toss it towards the wastepaper basket. It misses.

"Don't worry, I was just finishing up."

She hovers awkwardly in the doorway. She has the lithe, long-legged body of a dancer.

"My name is Sylvia Lloyd. I wonder if you can spare a few minutes of your time? I have a job I would like to discuss."

I gesture towards the swivel chair opposite me. It was salvaged from a skip, but it doesn't look too bad.

She sits down slowly, and gazes warily at the office walls.

One wall is plastered in press clippings for all of the cases I have worked on – at least the ones that ended well. Another wall contains photos of all of the missing persons that stayed missing. The wall behind me is blank apart from a faint blood spatter-pattern that has been there since a man called Clarence Clement pulled a knife on me two years ago. Admittedly, that had nothing to do with the day-job: I picked up his wife in the Dirty Lemon one Friday night.

I didn't realize that she was married, and I took my beating like a man. However, I felt that the knife was excessive, and I broke his arm in two places and pushed him down the stairs. The paramedics had to scrape him off the pavement outside the North Atlantic Video Lounge. I left the blood on the walls partly out of laziness and partly as a reminder of my own mortality.

I inherited the office from a disgraced ex-cop known as Wet-Look around four years ago. He was a bad man, one of the worst I have known. For some reason he left me the office in his Will – believed we were kindred spirits – on some level, at least. The only other things he left behind were an upholstery knife and a half-empty bottle of ulcer medicine, both of which I found in the top drawer of the desk.

I have been tracking down missing persons and other miscreants for around five years. It pays surprisingly well – even in a small town like Paignton.

Nowadays I turn down more work than I accept, and the only jobs I agree to take are the ones that I can't think of a good reason to turn down.

Sylvia unbuttons her trench-coat. Her leopard print blouse clings to her breasts. I'm ashamed to admit that she has my attention.

A shabby-looking fat man stumbles through the door, breathing heavily. He stinks of rotten cigarettes. His nose has been broken so many times he has to breathe through his mouth. It gives him an unfortunately slack-jawed appearance. I open the desk drawer and put my hand on the rubberized grip of one of my two claw hammers. I don't plan on getting stabbed in my own workplace again in a hurry.

Sylvia looks alarmed.

"Mr. Rey – this is my husband, Frank."

I drop the hammer, and slide back into my swivel chair. Jesus. My back feels slick with sweat. I look around for another beer, but come up short.

Sylvia passes me a photograph. The picture seems to be of her and another girl.

"My daughter: Priscilla. I was 15 when I had her – people say that we could pass for sisters."

I nod. She's very attractive. Full lips, strong chin, high forehead.

"Last week she was offered £300 for a photo session by two men on Winner Street. They had business cards, credentials. I encouraged her to go along."

"What happened?"

"She never came back. Frank went looking for her, but he asked the wrong questions in the wrong pubs. They broke all of his fingers and fractured his cheekbone."

I glance up at him and he grimaces, awkwardly. I stare at the press clippings on my wall instead.

"Any other distinguishing features?"

"She has a large tattoo of a black flower on her back. I never liked it."

Sylvia re-applies her maroon lipstick. It makes me feel slightly queasy.

I slide the photo into my desk drawer, next to the hammers, and take a deep breath.

"OK, I'll take the case."

"What's your daily rate?"

"Don't worry – I'm very affordable. We can settle up later."

She clasps my hand.

"Thank you, Mr. Rey."

I withdraw my hand.

"Don't thank me yet. Write your phone number down on this pad and I will contact you in one week or less. I'll be frank with you: if I can't find her within seven days she is probably already dead."

A solitary tear trickles down Sylvia's cheek. Frank's breathing becomes ragged and he vomits on the carpet.

The basement at Paignton police station has been painted brown so that the blood doesn't ruin the walls.

I'm not a cop. I'm not even a good man. But I am effective. Last year I tracked down a man that the press called the Plastician. He was responsible for the murder of six girls – four of them prostitutes. One of them was only eleven.

Carver — Detective Inspector Carver to his colleagues — used to hate my guts. Luckily for me, he has always hated the Triads more. I used to do investigative work for a mobster called Malcolm Chung — well before Carver's time — and that particular career move still seems to carry weight locally.

When a Cantonese girl was found in Palace Avenue Gardens with an eyeball stuffed in her mouth Carver offered me a commission to track down the men responsible. I delivered on my end of the bargain, and now we have a quid pro quo arrangement. He doesn't get in my way, if I don't get in his.

Simon Sloman is a methedrine addict. He has a tough face and a broken nose, but he is too soft for what Carver is about to do to him. The interview room stinks of ruined lives. I'm watching Carver through the scratched one-way Plexiglas. He paces the room like a caged animal, scratching at his acne scars. If I didn't know him I would think that he was the skell, not the cop. The ridge of scar tissue on the bridge of his nose twitches as he starts to talk.

"That wound looks like a breeding ground for bacteria."

"W-w-what wound?"

Carver lashes him across the top of skull with a

cosh. Simon's head cracks audibly and he starts to sob.

In the middle of the cement floor there is a metal drain. I have never noticed it before, but it doesn't take too much imagination to guess what it is for.

Simon crawls across the floor towards the door. He is cut, bruised and covered in sweat. Dark blood seeps into the concrete and oozes towards the drain.

A cigarette that is half-ash dangles from Carver's mouth and he pummels Simon again, harder this time.

I step back from the Plexiglas and slump against the wall. Carver grinds out his cigarette and lets himself out of the chamber of shrieks.

"You call that an interrogation?"

Carver shrugs.

"Where is his lawyer?"

"Not my problem. Milo Purvis is a surprisingly hard man to get hold of."

Carver lights another cigarette and hoists his feet onto the desk.

"You wanted to talk?"

He looks at his watch.

"I have five minutes."

Carver has a weird masochistic streak. Every Thursday morning he pays for a hand-job in Cantonese jack-shack, just to torture himself. He knows that I know, he just doesn't care.

I show him the picture and he grunts.

"The daughter is the one on the left."

"Obviously."

He sighs.

"The girl got snatched on Winner Street after a photo shoot. Any ideas?"

He clears his throat.

"I heard some chatter, but nothing concrete."

"What kind of chatter?"

"Rumours about a posse of rogue cops from out of town. Plymouth, maybe further afield. Working with some bad men. People trafficking and worse. They seem to have a penchant for pretty white girls. We raided the Intercontinental Hotel after an anonymous tip off, but didn't find any girls. Barely found any criminals."

"Doesn't Milo Purvis own that hotel?"

"A minority stake."

"How do you like that for a coincidence?"

He offers me a crooked grin, and swings his police-issue shoes off the desk.

"Coincidences are never a good thing in my line of work."

"They are in mine."

I walk out into the sun-blurred afternoon. I feel disorientated after spending so long in the basement. This summer has been so hot it sometimes feels like my blood is boiling, and today is no exception. I cut down Well Street, past the boarded-up funeral parlour. It still amazes me that a funeral parlour can go bust in a town like this. I'm gasping for a drink, but there are no shops left in this part of town. Instead I cut down Crown & Anchor Way and head across Palace Avenue. This street has a weird fucking smell that even I'm not used to yet.

The barmaid at the Dirty Lemon is new. She has bad tattoos and eyes the colour of spilled coffee. She offers me a pint of Stella and a sickly-sweet smile. It's a potent combination, and I decide to loiter at the bar and make small-talk.

"Is Terry around?"

"It's his day off. He's upstairs. Watching his videos."

I nod and take a long drink of my beer.

Videos? Who the fuck watches videos anymore?

The North Atlantic Video Lounge is the kind of place where bad people go in search of a good time. When I enter the shop it's quieter than a tomb – completely empty except for the emaciated desk-jockey behind the counter. He is sprawled across a swivel chair, holding a dog-eared copy of 'Tailgunner' up to his face, as if scrutinizing the images for minor deformities. He shifts in his seat when I walk in, but doesn't lower the magazine.

"If you're after a copy of 'Anal Annihilation 4' they won't be back until 6 o'clock."

I step forward and punch him in the face, through the magazine. He yelps in pain, and lowers the porno, grimacing through bloody teeth.

"What the fuck was that for?"

"Didn't your boss ever tell you that it's rude to ignore potential customers?"

"Mr. Balthazar doesn't give a shit how I treat customers."

Barry Balthazar. Someone needs to flush that man away like the greasy shit he is.

I'm picturing Balthazar's fat, sweaty face when I punch the desk-jockey for a second time. Carver's little floorshow at the cop-shop has left me feeling agitated. Excited, almost.

"What are you, a fucking cop?"

"No. I'm much worse than that."

He scrambles backwards towards the rusty filing cabinet, presumably in search of a bat or a blade. I wait until his hand is in the drawer and vault over the desk, slamming the cabinet closed on his wrist. He screams.

"Wrong move, dick-rash."

He slumps to the floor, rubbing at his arm. He's sweating like a bus station rent-boy between fixes.

"Fuck off, man. I haven't done anything wrong. Ask my fucking parole officer."

"You know what – I don't want to talk to your parole officer. I want to talk to you."

"Aw, man. Please fuck off. I'm just the hired help. You know that."

I withdraw the crumpled photo of Priscilla from my jacket pocket and hold it in front of his face. He shudders involuntarily and closes his eyes.

"I didn't do nothing to her. You gotta believe me."

I snap another punch into his jaw and this time his greasy head makes a dent in the plasterboard behind him.

"Where is she, shit-stain?"

"I don't fucking know, I swear! Milo only paid me to hold the fucking camcorder!"

I stomp him so hard I leave a footprint on his face.

Milo Purvis offers me a flabby chuckle and a cigarillo – in that order. He has an office on Palace Avenue, above a cheque cashing joint. It has been a long time since he was a practicing lawyer. He perjured himself a few too many times for comfort and got disbarred two years ago.

Up close and personal his skin looks like grey putty. I've heard rumours that he is suffering from a slow putrefaction of the kidneys, and it is clear that he is not well. He is sweating so hard that his suit looks like it has been dipped in Paignton harbour and put on wet.

Thanks to the cigarillos, the air in his room is barely breathable.

"How's your little brother, Milo?"

He chuckles again.

"Housebound. He hasn't got out much since that bullet burst his lung. But of course, you already knew that, didn't you?"

He smiles at me with diseased gums. I think that he's getting me confused with someone else, but I decide to play along. I beat his brother once, a long time ago, but I never shot him. I've never shot anyone – I prefer using knives and hammers to do my dirty work.

"Why are you here, Mr. Rey?"

"I'm looking for a girl."

"Aren't we all…"

I start to take the photo out of my pocket, when Meat-Rack drifts out of the gloom, limply clutching a pearl-handled revolver. We have history, and it isn't good. He smiles, weakly, and I see he has four teeth missing from his lower jaw. That is definitely down to me.

He smells of booze, piss and failure, and when he tries to pistol-whip me he almost misses.

"Is that the worst you got?"

Milo chuckles for a third time.

I sink to the floor and reach down into my boot for the hidden pig-knife. As I am about to grab the handle, Gilligan emerges from the corridor and whips me across my left cheekbone with a rat-tail sap. Shit. That's going to leave a mark.

I hear Milo Purvis start to chuckle again. That joke definitely isn't funny anymore…

I can feel warm blood trickling down my face. It runs into my mouth and I cough myself awake. I've been shot six times in my life. Sliced, but never stabbed. Whatever Gilligan and Meat-Rack did to me hurt far fucking worse, that's for sure. I finger a shallow bullet-groove in my thigh. Jesus. I don't even remember either of them shooting me. It doesn't hurt too badly, but my shoe is already full of blood. I try to stretch my legs but the crate is too small. What a fucking mess.

I hear the screams before I hear the gunshots. I try to kick my way out of the crate and it sends a sharp pain up my leg.

Carver has a sawn-off shotgun looped over his shoulder with a length of electrical cable. Gilligan is lying in a mangled heap, a coil of his intestines pulsing onto the carpet. His wet lips are contorted into a hideous dead smile.

Carver grins at me.

"I thought I might find you here, sunshine."

He looks drunk. Very drunk. His next shot takes Meat-Rack's his head almost clean off. I swear I hear Carver laugh.

"Did you find the girl?"

I shake my head and he looks visibly deflated.

"Can you walk?"

I try to respond, but my shattered teeth and busted mouth mangle the reply.

Carver hoists me off the floor, and my leg gives way immediately.

"Stay with me, kid. Stay with me."

My heart is pounding so loud that I don't hear the rest of the gunshots.

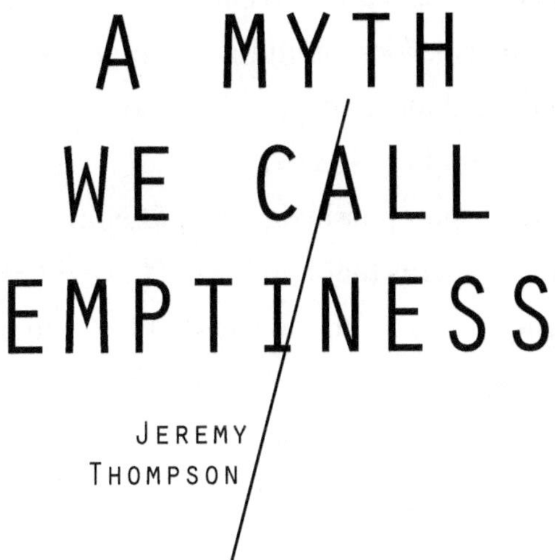

VI

That morning, a marker-scrawled message shrieked ANNIVERSARY from the dry erase board on Gail's refrigerator—red traced over with black, perhaps to obfuscate evidence of a trembling hand. Thirteen years to the day, it was.

Escaping the cityscape—and its twice-baked, putrefying garbage miasma, thick enough to chew—Gail journeyed to a miles-distant streambed, long-dried, whose malevolent ambiance had survived time's passage undiminished.

Rustling in gelid wind, weeping willows hem her in near-entirely, encompassing all but the pitted dirt road she'd arrived by. Jagged-leafed *Sambucus cerulea* specimens discard summer berries. Splitting in tomorrow's sunlight, they'll discharge blue-black pus. No insect songs sound. Perhaps the night has digested them.

Seated upon polished stones, listening for echoes of the liquid susurrus that had been, Gail exists—spotlit by headlights, oblivious to the fact that her station wagon's battery shall soon perish. Maliciously ebon is the night, an oily cloud penumbra shrouding the moon and stars.

Sucking Zippo flame into her cigarette, Gail wonders, *where is she? This was her stupid idea. What the fuck?* Wishing to be anywhere else but unable to budge, she listens for an approaching car engine, an erstwhile partner's arrival. *Why did I return to this loathsome site?* She thinks, nervously scratching her sagging countenance. *Why have I been dreaming of it? Why does phantom water make me shiver? Have I always been here…since that night? Am I finally to reclaim my lost pieces?*

Eventually, the distinctive sound of an unforgotten hatchback arrives. *Her 1980 Chevy Citation, still running after all these years,* Gail realizes, attempting to grin. *There's only one woman on Earth indifferent enough to retain such a vehicle. And look, here comes Valetta. Fuckin' wonderful.*

Claiming a seat beside Gail, the woman forgoes a

greeting to remark, "You put on weight."

"Perhaps I claimed what you lost," Gail responds, nodding toward a nigh emaciated frame, upon which a university-branded sweat suit withers. *Look at the poor bitch; she seems hardly there.*

Beneath her lined forehead, Valetta's eyes bulge gummy crimson. Sniffing back errant mucus, she pulls thinning hairs from her cranium, to roll between thumb and forefinger before discarding.

Should I hug her? Shake her hand? Gail ponders, uneasy. *She knows me better than anyone else ever will. That case made us soul sisters. Make that soulless. God, it hurts to see her pallid face again, her shattered intensity. I tried to forget it, along with everything, even myself. Did I come here to die, or to relearn how to live?*

Valetta pulls an item from her pocket, unfolds it, hands it over. "Remember us in those days," she asks, "so serious in our matching outfits, our shared delusion that justice existed?"

Finger-tracing the creased photograph, squinting sense from the gloaming, Gail confirms, "I remember." *Look at us,* she marvels, *in our black pantsuits and heels, our white blouses, crisp and neat. Even our figures had been comparable… somewhere between the two extremes we've become.*

We wore wedding rings then, installed by long-divorced

husbands whose faces are featureless on the rare occasions that I remember 'em.

After Gail returns the photograph to Valetta, the woman tears it into confetti that she tosses overhead.

"We considered ourselves innocents, when our births made us complicit in history's worst atrocity: humanity's proliferation," Valetta declares, sniffling. "If our race ever develops morality, we'll enter extinction that very day."

"Fuck you," Gail spits. "Why did you come here? Why did I?"

A moment implodes, then: "You know why. Idiotically, we thought they'd return."

Swallowing a stillborn gasp, Gail whispers, "The tepees."

"Thirteen years for thirteen of 'em. Numerology suggests significance in that number, you know…a karmic upheaval. Thirteen consumed the Last Supper. Thirteen colonies shat this country into existence. I began menstruating at age thirteen. Thirteen disappearances drew us here in the first place. Thirteen—"

"Yeah, I get it. You like numbers." Almost wistful, Gail hisses, "Do you remember them? The way they looked, lit from within as they were." *Human hair and tendons threading different flesh shades together,* she avoids saying. *The bones that kept the things upright: tibia, fibula, ulna and femur. Eyes, teeth, fingernails and toenails—thousands of 'em—artfully embedded in the flesh. Bizarrely silhouetted smoke flaps. The scent of…please, get it out of my head.*

"Always," Val answers, somehow grinning. "So terrifying, so…*beautiful.* The level of craftsmanship that went into each…a network of madmen and artists must have been working for years, symbiotically."

They've biologically ascended beyond their human components, Gail thought on that execrable evening, approaching the closest tepee. Her mentality was fevered, permeated with the unearthly. *Is it my imagination, or do they breathe as living organisms? Have such incongruities always existed? Did* Homo sapiens *devolve from them, long ago?*

In the festering city—where philandering husbands got their cocks sucked at "business lunches," and didn't even have the decency to wipe the lipstick from their zipper afterwards—exotic dancers of both genders had disappeared, too many to ignore. "Let the dykes have it," had been the chuckled decision, casting Gail and Valetta into an abyss of neon-veined desperation, where the living mourned themselves, being groped by the slovenly.

Their peers loved to crack wise. Being the only female detectives in the city, Gail and Valetta had heard 'em all. They'd partnered up to escape the crude jokes, awkward flirting, and unvoiced desperation of their male colleagues. For years, the two had pooled their intuitions to locate corpses young and old, along with the scumfucks who'd created then disposed of them. Occasionally, they'd returned broken survivors to society, as if those withdrawn wretches hadn't suffered enough already.

When Gail and Valetta began donning matching pantsuits, out of some vague sense of sisterhood that seems pathetic in retrospect, their peers had pointed out their wedding rings and labelled them spouses. They'd met Gail and Valetta's husbands. They said it anyway.

With doleful prestidigitation, Valetta conjures a second folded photograph and hands it over. Before unfolding it, Gail predicts, "Bernard Mullins."

"Who else could it be?" Valetta agrees.

Granting herself confirmation, Gail glimpses the self-satisfied corpulence of a strip club proprietor, able to fuck whomever he wished through intimidation. His sister was married to good ol' Governor Ken, after all, whose drug cartel connections weren't as clandestine as he believed them to be. Bernard's friends were well-dressed killers. His dancers barely spoke English. Even his bouncers had records.

From Bernard's four family-unfriendly establishments, thirteen dancers had disappeared over five weeks. Glitter sales went down. Everyone was worried. Enduring the man's reptilian gaze as it burrowed breastward, Gail and Valetta questioned him: "Any suspicious patrons lately?" Et cetera, et cetera.

As if spitting lines from a script, the man feigned cooperation and concern. "Well, nobody immediately comes to mind…but you're welcome to our surveillance footage. Anything I can do…*anything*."

"Fuck that guy," Gail declared, starting the car, minutes later.

"Let's surveil the pervert," Valetta suggested.

Days later, their unmarked vehicle trailed Bernard to a well-to-do neighbourhood. And whose rustic Craftsman luxury house did he enter, swinging a bottle of Il Poggione 2001 Brunello di Montalcino at his side? Good ol' Governor Ken's, of course.

The front door swung open, and Gail and Valetta glimpsed Bernard's younger sister, Agatha. With a smile so strained that her lips threatened to split, wearing an evening dress cut low to expose drooping cleavage, she hugged her brother as if he was sculpted of slug ooze. *One back pat, two back pat, get offa me, you pathetic monster*, Agatha seemed to think.

When he stumbled back outside hours later, Bernard's tie was looser. Sauce stained his shirt, a brown Rorschach blot. A clouded expression continuously crumpled his face, as if he'd reached a grim decision, or was working his way toward one. Returning to his Porsche Panamera, he sat slumped for some minutes, head in hands, and then returned the way he'd arrived.

The night seemed metallic, overlaid with a silver sheen. Passing motorists appeared faceless, unfinished, refugees from mannequin nightmares. Hearing teeth grinding, Gail wondered whom they belonged to, her partner or herself.

To Bernard's peculiar residence, an octagon house full of shuttered arch windows, they travelled, parking a few houses distant. On edge, Gail was sloppy about it, nudging a trashcan off the curb, birthing a steel clatter. Still, Bernard only glanced in their direction for a moment, and then unlocked his front entry. Minutes later came the gunshot, which summoned them inside, firearms drawn.

Aside from Bernard's crumpled corpse, the warm-barreled Glock in his hand, and the gestural abstraction he'd painted with his own brains, lifeblood and cranium, the house was empty: unornamented, devoid of furniture. Its parquet flooring and walls echoed every footfall, made every syllable solemn, as Valetta poked Bernard with the toe of her boot and muttered, "Serves ya right, you bastard."

After the funeral, they spoke with good ol' Governor Ken, who fiddled with his tie, trying on a series of expressions, hoping that one conveyed sorrow. "An absolute shock," he insisted, smiley-eyed. "He'd been so convivial at dinner. You'd never know he'd been suffering." Beside him, Agatha bounced the governor's eight-month-old son in her arms, cooing to avoid adult conversation.

Pulling photographs of attractive-if-you-squint missing persons from her jacket, Gail fanned them before good ol' Governor Ken, enquiring, "Recognize any of these good people?"

"Should I?" he responded, raising an eyebrow.

"They worked at Bernard's 'establishments,' and disappeared off the face of the Earth, seemingly. Did Bernard ever mention them to you, even in passing?"

Glancing to his child, his wife, then finally back to Gail, the governor replied, "Listen…in light of Bernard's profession, I'm sure that you'd both like to believe that I'm waist-deep in sordidness. But truthfully, he and I only ever discussed sports and musical theatre."

"Mr. Family Values," Valetta muttered, sneering.

Infuriatingly, good ol' Governor Ken winked at her. Without saying farewell, he escorted his wife to their limousine. "Don't touch me!" Agatha shrieked therein, assuming that closed doors equaled soundproofing. "No, I'm not taking those goddamn pills again!"

Watching the vehicle drive off, Valetta grabbed Gail by the elbow, and leaned over as if she was about to kiss her. "Remember when I went to the bathroom earlier? Guess what else I did." Pointing toward the limo, she answered herself with two words: "GPS tracker."

Glancing down at her hands, Gail realizes that this time, she's the photo shredder. Amputated features fill her grasp. Shivering, she tosses the confetti over her shoulder.

Eye-swiveling back to Valetta, she sees a third photo outthrust: an official gubernatorial portrait.

The drive spanned hours, interstates and side

roads. "He must have found the tracker and tossed it," Gail posited at one point. "Either that, or he's dead. Why else would his limousine be parked in the middle of nowhere for two days?"

Night fell as a sodden curtain, humid-glacial. Down its ebon gullet, they travelled. Gail's every eyeblink was weighted, her nerves firecrackers popping. Continually, she glanced at Valetta to confirm that she wasn't alone.

When they finally reached the limousine, they found it slumbering empty with every door open. Either its battery had died or somebody had deactivated the interior lighting. Shining flashlights, they spied bloodstained seats.

A baby shrieked in the distance, agonized, as if were being pulled apart, slowly. Seeking it, they discovered the streambed, whereupon thirteen tepees loomed. The centermost tent stood taller, sharper than the dozen encircling it. Black cones against starless firmament, they were scarcely discernible. Even before the flashlight beams found them, they felt *wrong*.

"Is that…human?" Valetta asked. For the first time since Gail had met her, the woman's tone carried no implied sneer.

Feeling ice fingers crawl her epidermis, burdened by the suddenly anvil-like weight of her occupied shoulder holster, Gail made no attempt to answer. A grim inevitability had seized her. Feeling half-out-of-body, as if she were being observed by thousands of night-vision goggled sadists—bleacher-seated, just out of sight—she slid foot after foot toward the nearest structure.

A cold voice in her head narrated: *Strips in all shades of human. Eyes tendon-stitched at their confluence points, somehow crying. Teeth, toenails and fingernails embedded…everywhere, forming patterns, hard to look at. Are they moving? Tepee designs replicate imagery from visions and dreamscapes, right? Didn't I read that, years ago? But where's the earth and sky iconography indicative of Native American craftsmanship? What manner of beings co-opted and desecrated their tradition?*

Inside…the tent's skeleton…arterial lining. Ba-bump, ba-bump. Is that my heartbeat? Where's that wind coming from? Is the tepee breathing?

She felt as if she should move, but it seemed she'd turned statue. Only after hearing her name called did Gail find her feet. Emerging, she saw the centermost tent spilling a misty indigo radiance from its open door and antleresque smoke flaps. Upon a pulped-muscle altar therein, a red-faced infant shrieked, kicking its little legs, waving its tiny arms. Somebody leaned over it, smiling impossibly, wider than his face: good ol' Governor Ken.

Whatever light source glowed purple, it suddenly

jumped tents. Now an elderly man—paunched and liver spotted in stained underpants—wiggled his tongue, spotlit. From a dark rightward tepee, wet-syllabled chanting entered Gail's ears. She turned to Valetta, but the woman was gone, her flashlight abandoned. Gail prayed to a god that remained hypothetical. Again, the light jumped. A nude crone exited a leftward tent—sagging breasts, oaken-fleshed—and then retreated as if she were rewound footage.

Something inhuman called Gail's name, then sang it with an unravelling tenor. Every tent self-illuminated, then fell dark. Numb-fingered, Gail groped for her firearm. Tripping, she shredded her knees, though the pain remained distant.

Replicated thirteenfold, the baby shrieked from every structure. Eye-swiveling from tent to tent as she stood, gracelessly mumbling, Gail felt a gnarled grip meet her shoulder.

Giggling, the old man frothed cold spittle onto her neck. Unseen hands began groping, as Gail's flashlight died. *Where are the stars?* She wondered, mentally retreating.

She awoke in daylight, a wide-eyed Valetta shaking her shoulder. The woman had sprouted fresh wrinkles. She seemed hardly there. The tents were gone, as was the limo.

Silently, they drove back to the city. Filing no reports, they watched their respective careers apathetically perish, along with their marriages, soon after. Eventually, they moved in together, to wallow in shared misery.

Realizing that they no longer lusted after men, they experimented with lesbianism one hollow evening, spurred by a bottle of red and several lines of coke. Dry and ugly, it was. Neither bothered faking an orgasm, as each would have seen through it.

Reporting more stripper disappearances, newscasters seemed amused.

Years fell down the bottle, as the world greyed and withered. Good ol' Governor Ken became grandfatherly Vice President Ken, champion for Christian values. Illegible graffiti sprang up everywhere, instantly fading.

One night, Gail pushed herself off the couch to find Valetta engaged in arts and crafts, constructing papier-mâché tepees from scissor-amputated ad features and scraps of anatomical diagrams. "I can't get it right!" she shrieked. "Help me, Gail! I can't stop 'til it's perfect!"

Impossibly, in the present, Valetta holds a tiny tepee composed of three shredded photographs. Giggling, she tosses it skyward. As the tepee unravels into mist, she enquires, "Do you remember last year? Do ya, Gail?"

Mad, Valetta had been, jittering, pulling her hair out. Muttering of a thirteenth anniversary, she'd vanished for days to parts unknown.

Awoken by living room thumping, a bleary-eyed Gail stumbled upon the unspeakable, a fugitive from a demon's bestiary. A crude imitation of the streambed tepees—reeking, rotting, dripping crimson—stood afore her, constructed from pet store fauna: birds, cats, rodents, dogs, fish, reptiles, rabbits and spiders. Something was wrong with its shadow. Furry, it wriggled across the carpet.

Licking her lips, the nude Valetta whispered, "Close, but no cigar."

"You killed me," Valetta says, and Gail relives it.

Terrified beyond rationality by her roommate's new hobby, hearing an infantile gurgling emanating from Valetta's tepee, Gail let instinct take over. Retrieving a steak knife from the sink, she rushed into the madwoman's embrace, jabbing and twisting until they both collapsed.

Awakening, Gail realized that Valetta and her tepee were absent, though bloodstains remained. Into the bottle, she retreated.

If the stars would only come back, everything would be fine, Gail thinks, in the present. Her car's battery dies, along with its headlights. Nearby, an infant shrieks eternally.

"Gail," Valetta says in parting. Widening impossibly, her eyes and mouth gush indigo luminescence. From ten digits, her hands spill matching radiance.

Arcing, the lights reach thirteen locations, trailed by Valetta's branching flesh. Exiting the pretense of corporality, the ex-detective twists—turning inside out, reconfiguring.

Becoming myriad eyes, teeth, nails, bones and flesh strips united by sinew and braided hair, Valetta's shade evolves into the abstract: thirteen tepees spilling indigo light. Each respires, and has a deafening heartbeat.

Unhesitant, Gail strides toward the centermost.

VII

MEDITATIONS

McKenzie Cassidy

{*Note: The following excerpt is from a composition journal found at the 3000 block of Orange Lane. The house, belonging to Mr. and Mrs. Ted Carmichael, was searched by police in connection to multiple homicides at East Smithville High School. Their son, Matthew Carmichael, who later died of the fatal injuries sustained from a gunshot wound, was named the primary suspect in the investigation based on footage downloaded from the school's closed circuit television system. Upon searching the private residence of Matthew Carmichael, with his family's consent, police found ammunition matching the calibre used in the shooting and a composition journal from which this text was taken. This is an abridged version of that text.*}

I can't wait to see the looks on the faces. Looks of horror, like the ones I got for years, but it's *my* turn now. They don't expect it, the Day of Reprisal, the role of it, *their final judgment*, but why would they? People are going to ask about it one day – ask about me – why and how I did it. So, here, I put my thoughts down on paper. I'm an extraordinary thinker. I can't even share all of my thoughts. The average human can't even understand me. They'll think I'm sick or evil, but don't we all suffer through life? That's what the Day of Reprisal is all about; a return to the void, the darkness, a loosening of the slack, a reclaiming of our essence that every "she" has taken away: our beings, our cocks, our lives. Society finds ways to harness us and it's time to break free, no hiding behind phony structures and deceptive adornments any longer.

I am reborn. This is the new me. Nothing will bring me back. I'd rather die before I let that happen, and I probably will by the end of it all. Andrea is first, no doubt, and the flaps of each girl taken, sliced cleanly from their filthy bodies. Cherokee warriors took scalps to mark victories over their foes and trophies of retribution, and that spirit will return again. She's long, bleached, and styled straight. I want it. I want to smell it. She'll beg me to stop and I'll remind her how she started it all. I told her that; but she spread that putrid twat anyway. She didn't listen and now I'll fuck her with a knife until she screams and understands. When judgment is upon her, upon them all, the strict sacrificial order will be followed: Natalie, second, and then Sarah, Julia, Melanie, and Brandi. Maybe they'll all understand how they led this to happen. How they hurt me first.

Sometimes I put the cold barrel across my cheek. I imagine a smooth bullet burrowing into flimsy skulls and grinding flesh like a steel hook through beef. They strut around, unconcerned, happy, dirty little assholes in the air like bitches in heat, fucked by degenerates spawned of society. They're so carefree; it makes me want to puke. I'm too smart for that. I know better. If they had figured me out than I wouldn't have to kill them all. They degrade their bodies and my treatment is a reflection of how they treat themselves. It's truly a gift for them. I get so excited that sometimes I picture jerking off – dick taut with thick blue veins pulsating in my palms – holding a gun to their heads, they watch me do it, screaming in their funny fucking faces. I get the joke now.

The media, the cowards, the liars, the sluts, the sell-outs, they'll ask how I did it? I'll share that now because I'm confident it won't fall into the wrong hands. Everything is ready. The fire alarm is too obvious and that trick's been done too many times. Doors will open like the great sword of the Archangel Gabriel cutting through limitations until my Day of Reprisal is complete. Once they lay out their defences, I'll follow my own grid to find every last one of them. Police response is too long and I'll have plenty of time. Clips hold 15 rounds, enough for six of the degraded and a few extra if I miss one or one bullet doesn't do the job, or if I need to hold off the police. I'll take fire from them, but it doesn't concern me because I have destiny and spirit on my side. They're incompetent and caught off surprise and can't understand the significance of the Day of Reprisal. It's my advantage. By the time I see them, it will have been done, and a success, and it won't matter if I'm dead.

This town and all of the fucked up degenerates living here will be talking about this day for generations. I know that now. The printed books that the children read, under The Great Day of Reprisal, will demonstrate how I transformed into the liberator. Choices matter and they made theirs and I made mine. They don't understand: I decide how good or bad it will be, not them. They made their beds, night after night after night with dirty dicks, and now it's time to lie in it. I will show them what choices they make. Many will ask if I felt sorry for what I did. No. Absolutely not. I'm doing a service to mankind and the universe, why should I feel sorry about that?

Think of me as you wish. All great men are misunderstood, until one day the populace recognizes their contributions to the world. I'm dead now. I'm proud to say that I died for a noble cause. I couldn't live a minute longer in this world, if that meant keeping my eyes shut or adopting the life of society's degraded. I'm not like them. I will now take my rightful place among great warriors and I ask the others out there, the silent like me, to rise up and show the new universe in all of its glory, before it's too late.

walk hand in hand into extinction

VIII

GRIEVING/IN REVERSE

DREW
CHIAL

ACCEPTANCE

Wind rattled the trees, clogging the gutters entire branches at a time. Rain spilled down the roof. The mansion's features were blurred beneath a cascade. All I could see were pillars and lights.

Behind the waterfall, the chrome plated doors looked like an art deco rendition of the Empire State Building. There were porcelain knockers on each of them. The one on the left was shaped like a comedy mask with a ring in its smile. The one on the right was shaped like a tragedy mask with a ring in its frown. I picked tragedy, or maybe the atmosphere picked for me.

A well-dressed man opened the door with hair like eagle feathers and a smile that buried his eyes in crow's feet.

He offered a manicured hand. "Mr. Advena? I'm Edgar Staples, assistant to Mr. Freeman."

Edgar regarded my yellow trench coat. "Please tell me there's a zoot suit under that."

"There's a zoot suit under this." I unbuttoned my coat to reveal a dress shirt, thin black tie, and pleated pants.

Edgar shook his head. "That's no zoot suit."

I pointed to the ceiling. "You said 'tell' not 'show.'"

He smirked. "I take it you were a screenwriter in a past life?"

I nodded. "And you?"

Edgar took my coat without answering.

I stepped out of the rain and onto a red carpet. The entryway was framed in footlights that lead to a box office window with an empty marquee.

Pulling a curtain back, Edgar led me through a leather door where I discovered, not the entrance hall of a grand manor, but the lobby of a movie theater. The bar was made up like a concession stand. There was a big neon sign where the *Let's All go to the Lobby* singers were joined by a smiling beer mug and martini shaker.

"Right this way." Edgar directed me to a flight of stairs with a golden railing up the middle.

"Aren't you going to ask me to shut off my cellphone first?"

Edgar gripped the railing. "Right after I show you the fire exits."

DEPRESSION

Ramsey Freeman was a short stout man, bald with a tuft of bangs, like Friar Tuck. He wasn't much to look at but he was a giant in the film community. His eyes were on the notecards on that famous corkboard, where he conceived *The Straw Husband*, *Mutiny on the River Styx*, and *We the Damned*.

The screenwriting professor at Columbia told us that Freeman plotted every scene on a notecard. The board fit seventy, no more no less. If Freeman had extra scenes it would force him to decide what to cut. Except today those cards spilled onto the wall. Was this his *Gone with the Wind*?

"You have a lovely theater Mr. Freeman." I announced myself.

He kept his eyes on the cards.

Stepping into the room, I realized he'd filled every

wall. Mixed into the cards, were parking stubs, G.P.S. print outs, photos of his late son Michael taking selfies at sunset, raising a glass with friends, and rocking the Wolverine claws with the hair and biker jacket that went with them.

I spotted a print of a cute Goth chick in a tank top with a sleeve of tattoos. She was checking her phone, oblivious to the photographer. I plucked it off the wall. The edge of the picture was blurred, the telltale sign of a telephoto lens.

"What is all this?"

Ramsey spun around. "The last month of my son's life." Charging toward the entrance, he tapped the wall. "From when he started his internship at Screen Constellations," he knocked on the opposite side of the frame "to the day they found his body in the lobby."

"I take it you don't believe the reports?" I examined the final photograph, the blackened body with the texture of bark, arms spread out like a scarecrow.

Freeman scoffed. "That my son burnt himself alive protesting the studio system? No, I don't." He flattened a satellite image. "No one at the construction site saw who took the gas, no one saw who poured it, and no one saw who ignited it."

Ramsey jabbed a black and white photo: a silhouette made of light with a Roman candle for a head.

"He was engulfed by the time the camera spotted him." Freeman traced a construction blueprint. "The arson unit combed the stairwells, the back halls, the bathrooms and they couldn't find the source of the ignition."

I shrugged. "Matches burn. Even lighters melt."

"Plastic melts at several hundred degrees higher than flesh."

Of course Ramsey knew that, the man was notorious for over-researching.

He unspooled a receipt. "Someone planning to kill themselves doesn't order a boom mic, a 750 watt lamp, and a green screen." He tapped a printout full of word balloons. "They don't text friends pitches for web series, hours before their deaths."

In my experience, suicidal people did all this. They ordered stuff, made plans, thinking they were giving themselves something to look forward to, like sharks in constant motion for fear of dying.

I nodded anyways. "So where do I come in?"

Ramsey tapped his thumbnail to his teeth. "A colleague told me you had a talent for finding information that wasn't..." he searched his cards for the words, "in the public domain. Berkley's been forthcoming, but the studio's been stonewalling. I need to know Michael's relationship with everyone he worked with."

"Where should I start?"

"There." Ramsey nodded to the picture of the girl in my hand.

Of all the exhibits on the wall, what made me reach for that one? Later I'd recognize the decision for what it was, the type of convenient coincidence writers can only get away with in act one.

BARGAINING

Ramsey had the parking manifest for Screen Constellations. He knew who every vehicle was registered to. The mystery woman wasn't among them. Edgar snapped the candid on her way out of the building. Uploading it into a Google image search came up with nothing, until I ran it against the headshots on IMDB.

Her name was Cassie, a screenwriter with three short films to her credit. Screen Constellations didn't have her on any staff listings.

She'd just dropped out of Berkley's film program, a degree so prestigious that that almost never happened. She was 22, which would've put her in Michael's class. A few calls under the guise of Academic Services revealed they'd been interns at Screen Constellations at the same time.

Tenants in apartment buildings ought to get to know their neighbors. I could've been anyone ringing the buzzer at nine at night.

"Sorry, I locked myself out again."

Once a stranger buzzed me in, I found Cassie's apartment, pulled out my wallet and started knocking. The door swung open before my knuckles hit wood. Cassie stood on the other side, jet black hair frizzy, eyes squinting, a lioness primed to pounce.

I jumped, almost unfurling my wallet to reveal the bus pass.

Cassie gave a coy smile. "I saw your feet."

There was only one vantage point that low and Cassie looked like she'd been there for a while. There was a carpet pattern on her cheek. She wore a long shirt and pajama bottoms, but it was clear she hadn't slept in days. The red of her eyes was framed by the bags beneath them.

I waved my wallet. "I'm here to ask some questions about Michael Freeman."

Cassie held the door open. Real detectives have partners, they're supposed to give their names and use permission statements, but sometimes when you speak with authority, people assume you have it.

Cassie's unit was a fire hazard. The hall, the shelves, and the kitchen counters were filled with stacks of paper. There were pages on the welcome mat, red with edits. By the formatting, I could tell they were screenplays.

The carpet was littered with bleeding ink cartridges. There was a printer and a laptop on the coffee table, where fresh reams waited beneath.

"It took them long enough to send someone." Cassie scooped pages off the love seat so I could sit.

I flipped my notepad open. "No one questioned you at the scene?"

She rolled her eyes. "I might have wandered away from that tired scene."

"Do you mind if I ask what your relationship was with Michael Freeman?"

Cassie fell across the couch cushions. "Relationship? We were interns. We read screenplays so the producers didn't have to."

I wrote "SCRIPT READER" on my notepad. "Tell me about Michael's last day on the job."

Cassie opened her fingers wide, pantomiming an explosion.

I kept my poker face.

She sat up with a smirk. "We'd finished grading the

solicited scripts, so we decided to dive into the Blacklist."

"Blacklist?"

"The Blacklist is a collection of screenplays that have high marks from readers, but will never get turned into features."

"Why?"

Cassie shot up to sift through her papers for a needle in a haystack. "They're fresh ideas in an industry churning out sequels, prequels, betweequels, remakes, reboots, and reimaginings. Why risk money on something new when you can resurrect the same ancient brands?"

From where I sat, I saw stacks all the way down the hall, through the bathroom and into the tub. None were bound. There was no clear filing system. I had a hard time picturing Cassie lugging a dolly full of reams up the steps.

Glancing back at my notes, I found I'd drawn a spiral on the pad. The decor was derailing my train of thought.

Cassie surgically removed a handful of pages from a stack. "If you're looking for a suspect. I'd start with The King in Yellow."

"The King of who?"

Cassie patted her pages. "Not who, what. *The King in Yellow* was the screenplay Michael was reading when the spark of inspiration hit."

Gripping the edges, Cassie wielded her bundle like a weapon.

"It was the only script he'd given a 5 out of 5. When he wandered off in a euphoric stupor, I knew I had to sink my teeth into it."

Cassie stared at her title page.

"Right out of the gate, the story was too outlandish. It was about a masquerade ball, in an otherworldly place called Carcosa, where the stars were black and twin suns shined underwater. There was no clear protagonist. No one's mask slipped long enough to reveal their motivation, just a graphic orgy of decadence."

Cassie giggled, a joke teller eager to get to her punchline.

"My notes were littered with potential breaks in the routine, when guests arrived, when they began the offering of skin, when the guards went missing, but I couldn't decide on one. Turns out the break was a character, an uninvited guest who'd infiltrated the plot."

She licked her Cheshire cat smile. "That bland first act is what makes the story so brilliant. It lulls you into a false sense of security before charging through the fourth wall."

I flipped my pad shut. "What do you mean?"

Cassie knocked a stack over, revealing a full length

mirror. She spoke through her reflection. "A good movie draws out your empathy. It tricks you into projecting yourself onto the hero, until their goals are your goals, their losses are your losses and their changes are yours. This script did the opposite. It imprinted itself onto the reader. When the fire alarms went off, I was evacuated before I could finish. It was gone when I came back." She waved her arms over the mess she'd made. "Now my story is incomplete."

Cassie set her script in my lap. The title page read:

THE KING IN YELLOW: ACT 3

The draft number was in the triple digits.

She got down on all fours to dig out something from under the couch. "I tried to find the script online. All I found was a collection of shorts by Robert W. Chambers, published in 1895. His book mentions the play, but contains fleeting excerpts. Chambers focused on the people who'd gone mad just from reading it."

While I debated flipping through Cassie's offering, my fingers decided for me. Skimming the text, I saw she'd written herself into the story. It read:

CASSIE

I still can't get the ending right.

A hammer COCKS. Cassie slides the 22 under her chin, the pistol barely peaks out of the shadow of her jawline.

THE KING IN YELLOW
Wait!

Cassie said, "I still can't get the ending right."

A hammer cocked. I looked up to find the situation playing out just as Cassie had written.

"Wait!" Tossing the pages, I went off script. "If you're trying to kill yourself, a 22 caliber is the wrong way to go. The bullet might not even breach the roof of your mouth."

Playing into someone's delusion is a long forgotten art form.

Cassie repositioned the gun to her temple.

I frowned. "25 percent of people who shoot themselves in the head survive."

Pressing the muzzle to her heart, Cassie waited for my approval.

I stepped through the pages, careful not to seem too alarmed. "You spent weeks writing and that's the best you can come up with?"

Tears welled up in Cassie's eyes. "I don't know how else to do it."

I cracked my neck. "Then we'll need to find the original for reference."

ANGER

The script didn't matter much to me. I wanted a closer look at the things Edgar couldn't capture with his telephoto lens, and an excuse to keep the gun out of Cassie's hands.

"Name please." The greeter was all silk scarves and shoulder pads, presiding over a table full of tags. Beyond her was the last Screen Constellations event in Cassie's calendar application.

I could've chosen to be anyone, but my hand reached for a blank tag. "I'm a stranger."

The greeter pulled it out of reach. "This is a staff event."

"He's my plus one." Cassie came in a formfitting pinstripe pantsuit. Her hair was slicked back, the bags under her eyes were hidden by mascara. She'd cleaned up nicely.

The greeter lit part way up with a smile that didn't reach her eyes. Cassie's name was nowhere near the tip of her tongue.

"Katie." Cassie chose a tag at random and we were in.

I'd taken snapshots of Ramsey's blueprints, I knew which stairwell would take us where.

When we got into the office, the script was where Cassie left it, wanting to be read. She hugged the pages, while I took pictures of a pack of cigarettes. The studio hadn't touched the desk since the incident. Turns out, Michael had an ignition on him the entire time. He just never bought smokes on any of the cards his father checked. The only mystery was his motivation.

Cassie cackled. Her madness trigger by the mere sight of the title page:

THE KING IN YELLOW

BY

ALAN SMITHEE

"What's so funny?"

Cassie traced the name. "Alan Smithee is the alias directors give when they disown a project. I can't believe I didn't spot it."

"Who'd use a pen name for an unsolicited script?"

"A messenger."

Cassie sniffed the paper as if to open her pallet. She offered it to me. "Don't you want to know what it says about you?"

I couldn't help but wonder if I had the mental resilience to handle what Michael could not. After all, his silver spoon had weakened his stomach, mine was hardened by the streets. What did I have to fear?

We stayed up there, a pair of moths circling a flame, reading, sharing skin, until we came to the realization that the story wasn't done.

Most screenplays are journeys to other worlds, this one was on its way to ours. We were the airport limo, the pages were our sign, and the Yellow King was our passenger. We had a responsibility to get him where he needed to go.

Buttoning her shirt up, Cassie studied photos of the construction site before going off to borrow some things. I gave her time to chain the doors, before I came down the elevator.

I don't care what my lawyer said, there's no such thing as temporary insanity, only clarity.

The executives outside the elevator had it easy.

Even with a 22, I'm an excellent marksmen. Those other charlatan storytellers weren't so lucky. When I emptied the clip I was forced to improvise. The stanchion holding the velvet ropes proved too inviting. Sure, it had a heavy base, but I didn't have to carry it alone. The Yellow King was wearing me like a mask.

Together, we left an impression on everyone.

DENIAL

The screenplay was a metaphor about everyone that would ever touch it, a paper reflection. In 120 pages, it had something on everyone. I saw myself staring back. I saw Cassie. I saw Michael. I saw a decadent industry brought to its knees. When you have a clear vision of Carcosa it looks into you.

Once the stars turned black and the lights rose from Lake Hali, my role was defined.

Somehow I knew the moment I touched that knocker on Ramsey's door, I'd been cast in a tragedy. Feeling it coming, I'd been grieving the entire time. The script knew how I'd try to deny it, like a set of finger-cuffs for the intellect, the more I resisted the more it tightened. Then Cassie sweetened the pot.

She made an airtight argument that freewill was an

illusion, showing her work, bringing me to a conclusion.

Mine is not a cautionary tale, it's an endorsement, a blurb on the back. Mark my words, *The King in Yellow* will come into your possession, that much is inevitable. You can put it through the shredder or take it to your armchair. The choice is up to you, but let's not kid ourselves, we both know that decision was already made for you.

walk hand in hand into extinction

IX

JACOB COUNTY

Mark T. Conrad

I ain't going to swear this is the truth. In fact, I know it's not *all* true. Some of it's made up for sure. But it gets to the point of what happened, what happened to these two boys, I mean. I didn't know them real well, just in passing, but I knew enough about them to put something down on paper, and I know what happened *to* them, and that's what's important. Though I ain't going to say how I know it. That'd be plain stupid.

You'd have to wonder how these two ever got paired up with one another—they was State Police Detectives, if I didn't say that. They were as mismatched as a blind man's socks on washing day. The one, Wade Wilkins—that wasn't his real name—I took to be a regular guy, family man, though he drank a fair bit, career officer, served in the military. His hair left him about the time his wife ran off, and his Army conditioning had gone to seed, leaving him with a paunch. Could've been a farmer or a truck driver, any of those fellows you see down at the Elks or the Moose club on a Saturday night, throwing darts and shooting the shit.

The other one, Freddy Hart, let's just say he'd read a few books, and he didn't mind letting you know. Funny thing was, he was more stick than Wade was, coming from Oaktown, West Virginia, just a stone's throw across the river from Jacob County. Whereas old Wade was city—he hailed from up near Columbus. His daddy was in real estate, I heard. Wade was bony and thin and some speculated he was on drugs, but I don't know. I think he just had some mental problems. Anyhow, he looked like the kind of guy you'd call scrappy, only he was too tall for that. Had pock marks on his face and smoker's teeth. He'd drum his fingers on his thigh whenever he got to thinking deep about something, which was most of the time.

The two of them picked at one another worse than a couple of old spinsters fighting over a quilt. They were too different in terms of outlook and disposition, and I wondered more than once if their Lieutenant didn't put them together as some kind of a mean joke.

They were investigating what was adding up to be serial murder—Freddy was convinced that's what they were looking at. The third body'd been found right here in Jacob County on state land. This is where these two run into Sheriff Leroy Thomas Bone, the law in Jacob and the kind of fellow used to being in charge. A big, powerful man, the Sheriff looked like he could whip just about anybody without breaking a sweat. For sure, he'd cracked a few heads since becoming a law man. People tended to be afraid of him, and that's how he liked it. Me, I say they had a right to be afraid.

Sheriff Bone only had the two deputies, not even enough personnel to secure the crime scene, so as soon as Wilkins and Hart showed up, first thing they did was call in for State Police Patrol cars to come and mark off the perimeter.

"Hold on one second," said Sheriff Bone. "Me and my deputies got this thing handled."

"The three of you?" said Wade, and he smirked, even though he shouldn't have.

That sent color into the Sheriff's face.

"Just hang tight here, Sherriff," said Freddy. "Officers are on their way. They'll give you backup to help keep this area clear."

They stood on the edge of a thick patch of woods

running off as far as you could see. The sun lay just on top of the rows of corn plants across the road. Flashers on the patrol cars lit up faces. You could hear crows in the treetops calling one another, like they were commenting on the scene below.

"You say the body's on back through here," said Wade with a nod at the clutch of trees.

Sheriff raised his chin. "Can't miss it."

"Your deputy told us some boys riding a minibike through here found the deceased."

"That's right."

"We'll need to talk to them."

"Whatever you want, detective," said the Sheriff.

Wilkins and Hart started into the woods, clicking on their flashlights as they went.

When they were out of earshot, the Sheriff turned to one of the deputies. "Get on the radio," he said. "Call the state police and have them call back those prowlers. We don't need them."

"Right away, Sheriff," said the Deputy.

Wilkins and Hart tramped through the underbrush, sweeping flashlight beams left and right. Those woods get humid, and sweat beaded on their foreheads. Wilkins kept slapping at bugs, left and right, but they didn't seem to bother Hart.

"You oughtn't have done that," said Freddy.

"Done what?"

"Laughed back there."

"What, at the bumpkins?"

"This is what I've been telling you, Wade. You lack insight into people. You have no psychological acumen whatsoever."

"Bullshit, I got no insight into people."

"That's why you'll never be a true detective."

Wade looked over at him in the fading light. "Yeah? That's what makes a true detective—psychological acumen?"

"That, along with reason and observation. You learn to observe what others don't see, to pick up the clues. Reason helps draw the thread of causality from those bits of information left behind back to the necessary unfolding of events. And a keen grasp of psychology allows you to determine motive and find the perpetrator. It's as simple and perfect as a quadratic equation. Solve for x."

"It's as neat as math, huh?"

"It is, as long as you have a firm grasp of the true nature of humanity."

"Which is what?"

"Man is a predator, born to hunt, to overpower, to consume what he desires, even—and I'd say, most especially—his fellow man. People live to prey on one another—that's what we're genetically designed to do. Their motives are as predictable as any stone rolling down a hill."

"You know, Freddy, I'm surprised you don't have any friends, with as sunny a disposition as you got? Jesus, man, life of the fucking party—that's what you are."

"The truth is ugly, as Nietzsche once said."

Their path led them to an opening in the trees carpeted by a layer of soft grass and leaves. A circle in the middle of the area some six feet in diameter had been burned into the grass. The body lay, limbs outstretched, in the center of the circle, like one of Da Vinci's human figure drawings. The flesh had been stripped from the corpse, but it was still identifiable as belonging to a woman.

"Number three," said Wade, jotting down notes.

Freddy knelt down to have a look.

"Ligature marks on the wrists and ankles," he said, pointing. "Same as the others, only they're cleaner. Must have been tighter, done faster, so she didn't struggle as much. He's improving."

"Should've brought a lantern," said Wade, wiping sweat and glancing around at the encroaching darkness. He could just see the circle of trees at the perimeter and nothing beyond.

"Also, looks like the razor cuts are smoother, less hesitation," said Freddy.

"So what's that tell you, Mr. Psychological Acumen."

"Tells me our predator's got a taste for this work and he's getting better at it."

"Yeah? Genius. My retard cousin could've come up with that conclusion."

Freddy stood, brushing off his hands.

"What would your retard cousin say about the fact that none of the three victims had pierced ears?"

Wade looked over at him.

"They didn't?"

Freddy shook his head, though Wade could hardly see him do it in the dark.

"German Baptists?"

"Could be," said Freddy.

"Means we've been looking in the wrong places to find where our victims came from."

"Also begs the question of why these girls weren't reported missing."

"All right, that's not bad," said Wade.

"What's that fellow's name, one in forensics, who talks about his German Baptist relatives?"

Wade looked up at the tree branches overhead. "Steinhaus."

"Right, Steinhaus. Let's talk to him, see if he can give us a way into that community, some kind of liaison."

"Listen, I'll tell you what makes a true detective," said Wade. "And it ain't no psychological acumen."

"All right. What is it then?"

"Gut instinct. It ain't no more than that. You can sharpen instinct with training and experience, but it has to be there in the first place, otherwise, you need to find yourself another occupation."

"Instinct, huh?"

Wade slapped his own cheek and examined his palm for the bug. He'd missed it.

"Yep. Nothing more than that. Psychology's horse shit."

"Horse shit, huh? You want to know what my psychological acumen tells me about you?"

Wade grinned. "I can't wait to hear this."

Freddy turned towards him.

"Tells me you're one highly insecure individual, always looking for something to give you confidence, either the job or some piece of ass you meet at a bar or the bowling alley."

Wade scoffed and started to say something.

"Let me finish," said Freddy with a wave of his hand. "You're an only child, and I'd bet top dollar that one or both of your parents were alcoholics—most likely both. Daddy didn't abuse you physically, but he sure as hell ran you down every chance he got. Whenever Daddy got rough with Mommy, she sought solace with you, didn't she?"

Wade's jaw hung slack. "Fuck you."

"Your ex-wife and your kids couldn't fill that void at the center of your being, so you fall desperately in love with every Jenny wearing lipstick, don't you, Wade? You're always hoping they can make you feel like a man, instead of a whinny little boy."

"Fuck *you*, and what you think you know about me and my life."

"Like I said, truth is ugly. It ain't easy having somebody hold a mirror up to you, so's you see yourself for the first time."

"You know, I'm glad we're finally having this conversation," said Wade in the darkness. He held his flashlight pointed to the ground. "Gives me a chance to express what I think about you."

"Be my guest."

"Your soul is sick. It's all shriveled up. You don't know nothing about love or friendship or happiness, or anything thing that gives a man pleasure or fulfillment. You probably never had a real friend. All you got is hate— for yourself most of all, but also for the rest of the world, because you can't stand yourself. You like to think of it all as some big existential statement, some philosophical position on the human condition, but really, Freddy? You're just sick in the head, *emotionally* sick."

"Well, shit, Wade, your retarded cousin could've come up with *that* diagnosis."

"Yeah, and when somebody calls you on your bullshit, all you got is some witty comeback like that. You never want to take any kind of a hard look at yourself, 'cause you'd see what a piece of shit you are."

Freddy swung his flashlight beam over, so it hit Wade in the face.

"I guess we're both fucked up," he said. "Maybe we deserve one another."

Wade let out a chuckle, shading his eyes. "Yeah, maybe. Now get that light out of my face."

Freddy lowered the beam.

"Let's get on back to the car and see what the hell's taking those cruisers so long."

"Yeah, and we got to get the ME and evidence team out here."

They heard movement in the woods and saw a

lantern coming towards them.

"'Bout time you all got here," Wade called out.

When the light and noise arrived at the edge of the clearing, they saw Sheriff Bone appear, not State Troopers. The Sheriff had a blue steel automatic pistol in his hand, pointed at the two of them. Beside him, coming into the light, stood a hulk of a man in overhauls, with a boyish, misshapen face.

"These here are the two I was telling you about," said the Sheriff.

The hulking boy-man grinned and raised his hand. He held a straight razor.

walk hand in hand into extinction

X

THE MAN WHO COLLECTED CHAMBERS

WILLIAM TEA

"Have you seen me?"

I'm looking right at her, but, no, I haven't seen her. Doubt I ever will.

She has pigtails and a warm smile. A stuffed animal is clutched tightly to her chest. There's a staple sticking through the top of her head.

My eyes move away from the girl and scale the rest of the taxi service's front window. She's not alone. The glass is wallpapered with flyers for missing persons. More than a few are children. It's depressing, but not unexpected after all this city's been through as of late.

It gives me an idea. Something about a creature on the loose in New Orleans in the aftermath of a hurricane.

Looking around, it seems like this would be paradise for a predator. People going missing left and right in the storm, who would notice a few more? Maybe I can tie it into the local Voodoo culture somehow. I whip out my moleskin and jot down a few notes. Hope I can turn 'em into something later on. Filler for my next collection, if nothing else.

This whole trip is treading dangerously close to being a waste of time.

"I've got some good news and some bad news," the lawyer on the phone said. The good news: Deacon Steen is dead, and he's left his entire collection to, "someone who'd appreciate it," i.e. me. The bad news: The storm that claimed Deacon's life had destroyed his home, including his library. The collection was in shambles.

"I'm sorry, there's nothing that can be done," the lawyer said. Said I was welcome to come down to New Orleans when the clean-up was done to salvage whatever was left, but ultimately the executor of the will didn't have any responsibility for the state of the inheritance in instances of "acts of God."

Nothing to be done? Hell there isn't. Wait for the clean-up? Yeah, wait for some piece of shit to get one good look at some dead famous author's house and decide to loot it, then make off with what rightfully belongs to me. No, I'm not wasting any time. I have to get over there now.

I have to find *The King in Yellow*.

"Fiction is a fabrication that reveals reality."

I waited for the applause to die down before continuing.

My third novel, *Widows of the Gyre* had met with modest-at-best sales, but I hardly cared about the tastes of the mainstream book-buying public. They were too busy drowning themselves in the banality of Jane Austen-meets-zombies pop-art mash-ups and jumbo-sized shock tabloids trying to pass themselves off as 'true crime novels' to delve into the caustic nightmares of legitimate literary horror. Those who knew something about the genre knew my work and appreciated it, so much so that *Widows of the Gyre* was in contention for several "Book of the Year" awards.

So it was that I was asked to appear as the guest of honor at New Orleans' Weird Menace Con. I even had my own Q&A panel: "A Mirror Darkly: Horror as Human Reflection, with Quint Megan."

As the claps subsided, I finished my thought.

"Storytellers use lies to tell the truth. The best horror fiction, real horror fiction, isn't just a mélange of gory descriptions and supernatural implausibility. By nature, horror and weird fiction are symbolic genres. No other genre has the gall to use symbolism as a scalpel to cut away the layers of self-deception we sift through every day as much as horror. Some people think of horror as escapist entertainment, but it's just the opposite. Truth is ugly, and horror is ugly. Thus, horror is the truest of all genres of fiction."

More applause. More cheers. I took a sip from the water bottle that had been left for me.

"Okay," the moderator beside me said, "let's open it up for questions."

An overweight man stood up, hand raised over his head. The moderator pointed to him. He mumbled something about "influences" which I took to be the same question I'd heard a thousand times before, and began reciting my stock answer.

"I'm influenced by everything, and I don't just mean everything I've read, I mean everything. Daily life, the news. The genesis of *Widows of the Gyre* was the persecution of Muslims in America that continues even today. Having said that, I'm most attracted to the bleak worldviews of classic weird and dark fantasy storytellers like Lovecraft, Blackwood and Machen. Thomas Ligotti is probably the best living writer working in the field today.

"If I had to point to one writer as a major influence, though, it'd have to be Robert W. Chambers. I'm a rabid collector of his work, completely obsessed. I actually spent the first advance from *Widows* on a rare German edition of *The King in Yellow* stories. For those unfamiliar, Chambers was mid-19th century author whose masterpiece was a collection of short stories, *The King in Yellow*.

The King in Yellow is also the title of a fictional play, featuring a pallid-masked mystery man in yellow robes. The play is a device that links many of Chambers' stories together, and both it and the masked man act as harbingers of madness and misfortune. Chambers' stories are about peeking behind the mask, literally, and finding something monstrous there. Here, those who pursue the truth rarely find happiness as a result, and that's something I've always felt; the truth, as I said earlier, is ugly. But the pursuit of it, however harrowing, is a necessary journey for all of us."

Later, after the panel was over, I sat at my table, signing copies of my book for fans when a familiar voice mumbled something to me about Robert W. Chambers. I looked up, and it took a minute for me to recognize the fan as the fat man from the panel.

"I'm sorry," I said, "what?"

He looked flustered, and took a moment to compose himself. When he spoke this time, he did so slowly.

"I said my name is Mark. I was at your panel earlier today. Um, I just wanted to say I loved it, and I'm really looking forward to reading *Widows*. And, um, you said you like Robert W. Chambers? I was wondering if you were familiar with Deacon Steen."

My brow furrowed. Steen was a trash-peddler who'd made a name for himself in the early '90s with sub-splatterpunk biographies of serial killers, with lurid titles like *Blooddrunk* and *Cannibal Metropolis*. I looked across the room to Deacon's table. The line of fans before him was short. His heyday had long passed. As I understood it, he was invited to Weird Menace every year simply because he lived in New Orleans anyway.

I turned back to the fat man, tried to seem interested.

"Oh really?"

He nodded. "I read an article once that said he had a huge collection of old books, like all kinds of rare stuff, all old-school horror. And I remember him saying in the interview that he spent most of his time tracking down Robert W. Chambers stuff."

Deciding it couldn't hurt to feel him out, I took a

break from my table to talk to the man myself.

"Hello, Mr. Steen."

I extended my hand to him. He didn't even look up, just signed a copy of one of his books, something called *Ghoul Feeding*, and held it out to me. I paused, unsure of what to do.

"Oh… no thanks. I've already read it. I'm, Quint Megan, I-"

"Ah yes, the guest of honor," he interrupted. He looked up at me at last, peering blearily through his Coke-bottle glasses. He smiled. "Sorry about that. After sitting here long enough, you start to become like an automaton."

"It's fine."

"I have to tell you, I really enjoyed *Widows of the Gyre*. Loved the shades of Frank Long and Bill Hodgson. And your previous two books were fantastic as well."

"Oh," I said simply, genuinely surprised. Perhaps Deacon Steen did indeed know a thing or two. "I didn't know anyone had read those at all."

Deacon chuckled and smiled up at me. I suddenly felt an obligation to return the compliment.

"It's an honor. I grew up a big fan of yours," I lied. "*Ghoul Feeding* was so… extreme. It's almost hard to believe it's a true story."

Deacon's face suddenly changed. His smile stayed,

but it showed hollow.

"There's no such thing as a true story," came his reply.

Corpses. They try to hide them under tarps, but that only makes it more obvious, more grotesque. The imagination works terrible wonders.

"I thought Louisiana graveyards were designed to prevent this sort of thing," I say to the taxi driver.

He doesn't look back at me when he replies. Doesn't look out the side window to see what I'm talking about. He already knows, doesn't want to see it again, just keeps his eyes glued to the road in front of him.

Or maybe he's just a very responsible driver.

In any case, this is what he tells me: "They are. Ya gotta have the crypts above ground, 'cause of the sea level. When it floods, that's usually good enough to keep them bodies from comin' loose and floatin' out to meet ya. But this storm, brother, this wasn't no normal storm. Nobody was ready for this one."

What seems like miles of caution tape separates the cemetery from the street. Without it, you can't tell where one ends and the other begins. There's at least two feet of water everywhere, and enough refuse floating in it to build a house. It occurs to me that much of that refuse probably comes from people's houses; all this rubble is the debris of countless shattered lives.

On the other end of the yellow tape, tired volunteer workers trudge through the water in waist-high waders. Some carry large rocks, chunks of what used to be gravestones. Most tend to the humanoid shapes under the tarps. They're lined up in the farthest part of the cemetery, where the water is at its lowest, and where they're farthest from the small army of curious children gawking from the roadside.

Two workers are carrying another tarp-covered shape to the end of the line on a makeshift stretcher. I watch as one end of the yellow tarp comes loose from under the shape and dangles down to the ground. I see where this is going, and my first instinct is to reach out and grab the flapping fin of fabric, but of course I'm so far away, inside a moving cab. The reflex is rendered ridiculous.

One of the men steps on the dangling tarp, and the whole thing tears away from the shape, revealing it to be the corpse we all knew it was but were hoping to forget. The man trips and falls back into the water, and the body comes tumbling after. It lands hard, rigid limbs twisting and splashing. It looks almost fresh, flesh withered and eaten away by rot but features still identifiable. The lips are gone, leaving a mouth full of teeth to form a hideous grin. Strangely, he's not wearing formal wear, nothing you'd expect anyone to be buried in. His clothes, though wet, ragged and dripping with filth, are visibly casual: a hooded sweatshirt and… are those waist-high waders?

The children at the edge of the caution tape see it all, but they barely react. They just watch on in wide-eyed silence. For the first time, I notice a man standing among the children. How could I have missed him before? He towers above them, tall and thin, a stark silhouette in his dirty yellow raincoat. His hood is up and his back is to me, so I can't see his face. He begins to turn towards me, and I'm struck by the paleness of what little I do see, but then the taxi turns a corner and the man in the raincoat, and the entire charnel scene, vanishes like raindrops cast aside by windshield wiper blades.

"Bullshit."

"I shit you not."

"Bull-fucking-shit!"

"Nope."

"I envy you," I said, "Sounds like one hell of a collection."

Deacon beamed at me through the paper-thin slit between his heavy eyelids, a vision of inebriated pride. I ordered us another round from the hotel bar, put it on the Weird Menace tab. I was guest of honor, goddammit. I'd earned it.

"You should come out sometime, to my home." His words were a smear of melting vowel sounds. "It's rare to meet someone who appreciates all that I've acquired."

After the book signings were over, I'd offered to take Deacon out for drinks. Hoped to pick his brain about his apparently massive collection of classic weird fiction. The drunken oaf was more than willing to boast. He claimed to have first editions and rare foreign versions of numerous classics, most notably Chambers' *King in Yellow*, *The Maker of Moons*, *The Mystery of Choice*, *The Haunts of Men*, and *The Tree of Heaven*. And though I doubted some of what he told me, the more we talked the quicker I came to the conclusion that I had to see this collection for myself.

I'd make myself his best friend and biggest fan if I had to.

"You know what, I'll tell you something I don't tell anybody," he said, his words broken up by a gasping, wheezing laugh. "I have something that nobody else has in the world. I have *The King in Yellow*."

He was drunker than I thought.

"What are you talking about?" I asked. "A first-edition? You already told me about that. I have one too-"

"No, no, no. You don't understand. I have the actual *King in* goddamn *Yellow*. The play!"

"What? That doesn't exist. It's like the *Necronomicon*, it's just—"

"Yes it does, trust me. It exists and I have it. Chambers, he wrote it. He wrote a lot of it, more than just the excerpts he quoted in the shorts. But he never finished it. It's a manuscript. Mostly just notes. But it's the Holy Grail. And I have it! Ha-ha!"

I remember looking down at my palms when Deacon had gone to the bathroom. There were indents in them of my own fingernails from how hard I'd clenched my fists, thinking that the greatest unread masterpiece of weird fiction might be locked away from the world by this drunken hack.

The sound of the Taxi tires slicing the skin of water that covers the ground stays with me long after my ride has gone and I've found my way into the battered manor that once belonged to Deacon Steen. I'd been here twice before (he'd been happy to show off every item of his collection, except of course, his supposed "Holy Grail"), but you could've fooled me. It's dark, the light outside fading behind a blanket of bruise-purple clouds, and the shadows are so solid they seem part of the structure itself.

I'm up to my knees in floodwater, and my hopes of salvaging something of value from my ruined inheritance are drowning fast. The beam from my flashlight cuts through the deepening black, shows me glimpses of walls with flaking painting and shattered windows like mouths ringed with broken teeth, choking on the bent and broken storm shutters that failed them.

All the opulence Deacon bought with the blood-money from his exploitative serial killer potboilers is now gone. The mask has fallen and the decay that always lurked behind is now laid bare. Part of me surges with righteous delight, even as another part mourns that which I likely have lost because of that unmasking.

I make my way to the library anyway.

The bookshelves are nearly empty. The glass cases in which Deacon kept his most valuable volumes are all either broken and empty, or toppled and floating. Amorphous globs of gray pulp bob in the water, or stick to the walls like parasites. It takes a few moments to realize those blobs used to be books. It seems Deacon's entire collection of rarities, amassed over the course of years and at the cost of more money than I or any of my books is likely to make in my lifetime, has been reduced to this.

I frantically scan the titles that are still on the shelves, hoping to find something that can be saved. I grab a first-edition M.R. James, but it falls apart in my hands. My fingers are left tangled in tatters of damp binding. I let them drop to my feet, but when the sounds of splashing has subsided, I notice another sound. A rushing, dripping sound. I follow it to the bottom of the bookshelf. I can see it now, in the yellow glow of my flashlight. All the water in the room flows here, and disappears. As if there were a hole or crack just behind the shelf.

The thing is damn heavy, and the floodwater doesn't make it any easier to move, but I manage to push it out of the way to reveal a moveable panel in the floor. Deacon, you squirrely bastard!

I pull the panel away, and a torrent snakes around my feet and pours into a compartment holding a water-tight lockbox. It's heavy, almost as heavy as the bookshelf, but I manage to lug it out of the alcove and onto a nearby desk.

I puzzle over it for a moment, all manner of thoughts warring for dominance until I finally settle on figuring out how to get the thing open. I pull out the envelope the lawyer sent me with the keys to the house in it. Surely Deacon wouldn't put the key to his secret lockbox on the same ring that held the one to his garage, would he?

Yes! He did! One of them fits!

The metal box swings open. Inside I find first-edition copies of Deacon's own novels, which I hastily toss over my shoulder into the floodwaters where they belong. There are a few other items whose value escapes me: a yellow raincoat, a pair of black gloves, an old Polaroid camera. But underneath that, a thick manila envelope. My fingers scramble to tear it open and, oh god, I can't believe it! Inside, an archivally preserved sheaf of papers. Ancient and brittle, each one is individually filed in a separate envelope of clear plastic. I recognize the handwriting from my studies as that of Robert W. Chambers. And the text, I recognize that too: "Along the shores the cloud waves break / The twin suns sink behind the lake / The shadows lengthen / In Carcosa."

But there's more. I keep scanning, reading passages I'd never read before: "Cassilda and Camilla dancing in the light of the moon, the Phantom of Truth drawing queer symbols in blood, an inedible banquet of alien fruits on the banks of Hastur."

As I rifle excitedly through the pages, something

falls out from between them. I look down and find several Polaroids floating face-down in little circles around my ankles, like children playing ring-around-the-rosie.

I put the manuscript back in the box and bend down to pick one up. Just before I turn it over, a thought occurs to me: Why would Deacon leave the key to his greatest treasure, his hidden treasure, on his keyring? Unless… he wanted me to find it. Unless…

The photograph seems to glow in the beam of my flashlight. Nausea churns my stomach as I see tiny little bodies wrapped around one another. Angry welts on fragile young flesh. Black eyes, wet with tears. Dry, red wounds and wet, pink openings. One of them has pigtails and a mouth that I keep thinking should be turned up in a warm smile. But there are no smiles. There's no staple in her face this time either.

Of course, there's no way it could be her. She only just went missing, I think, and these pictures are old. My head is spinning like a bicycle tire. I can't think straight. Thoughts are colliding, merging together then pulling apart.

From the next room, I hear the sound of water sloshing in a steady rhythm. The rhythm of footsteps. Without thinking, I turn off my flashlight, gather up the Polaroids and the manuscript and shove them all back into the envelope, and make for one of the windows. Jagged glass teeth bite into my hands as I strain myself through. For a second, I think I see a flash of yellow and a pale face, but then I'm out and scrambling through the mud.

I burned the photos and kept my prize. *The King in Yellow* is mine.

I can't help think, though, that it's just a story.

All stories are stories. Maybe lies don't tell the truth. Maybe they just lie.

Maybe everything I've ever written has been just an obscuration of reality, not a revelation. Stories don't reveal harsh truths. They can't. That's not their function. They cover the truth up. Make it sweeter. Softer. Easier to live with. We live with the truth by escaping it, and pretending we're facing it.

Every story is a lie. Even this one. Especially this one.

Truth is speaking to us all the time, telling us things, asking us things. And the worst thing it asks is this: "Have you seen me?"

We should only answer, "No."

walk hand in hand into extinction

148

Denny "Slim" Reuthe was in prison shape. It started as a defense mechanism after his first state-mandated vacation. In Slim's world skin color wasn't an issue. Slim was white. His best buddies, Nate and Alex Colorundo, were Hispanic; no one gave a fuck.

In jail, though, it mattered. So, when Slim started mixing up his social circle inside, the Aryans singled him out as a race traitor. They caught him in the shower room. Broke three of his ribs and carved a rope of swastikas down his back—later Slim's tattoo artist, Animal, would morph the embarrassing scars into stitches being pried open by the mottled hand of a demon.

Slim made sure it never happened again. After his

release, he stocked up on protein shakes; gorged on meat. The cash Marco gave him for running pills went straight to a monthly membership at the Iron Men CrossFit gym—which was where he earned the ironic nickname Slim.

Somewhere along the way, though, it became less about throwing off the bad motherfucker vibe and more of an addiction. He loved the soreness; loved how the veins in his biceps bulged underneath the skin like bloated caterpillars. Slim could deadlift 200 pounds without thinking about it and bench press any of his girlfriends.

The lifestyle made him untouchable. The tattoo on his chest read PAIN = ME and Slim lived by that belief. There was nothing he couldn't destroy. Which was why, when Detective Salazar and her partner, left Slim alone in the interrogation room with the device bolted to the table, he didn't know if he should laugh or start sweating.

The device itself sat on top of a steel box. It was clear glass molded in the shape of a blender packed with tangled wires. The front panel was made up of three dials and a keypad. Embossed onto a small metal rectangle was the word: Interrogator. Two wires tipped with electrodes snaked from a port in the side.

Slim looked over at the glass window, certain the detectives were watching him.

"Fuck is this shit? Some kind of high-tech torture device?"

The speakers above crackled. A microphone whined.

"Please attach the electrodes to your temples, Mr. Reuthe," Detective Salazar said.

Slim crossed his arms. "I know my rights. You can't hurt me. Maybe you should, though. I could make some decent money suing you motherfuckers."

Deputy Sachs, overweight, underpaid, and too apathetic to wipe off the hot sauce dotting the front of his uniform, must have been posted right outside, waiting for an excuse. The door bounced off the wall. Slim ended up bound and bleeding from a split lip. Sachs placed the electrodes onto his temples, tapped the keypad, turned the dial up, and left.

"This would have been easier if you complied."

Slim looked around the confined space. The voice sounded close, as if it came from someone sitting across from him. The Interrogator must've had speakers hidden inside it. Still, it was eerie. Smoke filled the glass contraption. Firecrackers of light went off inside.

"Do you know why you're here, Mr. Reuthe?"

"I have no idea."

"Do you know Lenny Waters?"

"Never heard of 'em."

"What about Wendy and Justin Waters?"

"Nope."

Fog filled the Interrogator. Flecks of orange light winked inside the swirling grey mass. It crept out from the top, curled its way toward Slim. His mind told him it was just smoke, but instinct told him to run. He made a half-assed attempt to turn his face away, failed. Smoke invaded Slim's sinuses. The electrodes at his temples burned.

The concrete walls melted away. Slim was in the corner of his parent's garage, watching as a younger version of himself pace back and forth. Nate, clad in a long hatchet man t-shirt, and baggy jeans tried to keep pace with Slim.

"Dude, listen. It was a mistake. He's drunk. He didn't mean anything by it."

"Fuck that." Slim jammed a thick finger into his closest friend's chest. "He thinks he can just talk to Eliza like that? He's disrespecting all of us acting like a god damn fool. Call him in here."

"Slim, he's my brother. I'm not gonna do that."

All it took was a simple shove against the garage door and Nate returned with Alex in less than five minutes.

"What's up, man?" Alex didn't seem to think he'd

done anything wrong. He had that airless sway that only happy drunks get.

When Slim finished destroying the garage with Nate's brother, like he was a human baseball bat, he remembered feeling euphoric. Now, looking back, he only felt the guilt that had been percolating for years.

"Is this how you solve all your problems, Mr. Reuthe? With violence?"

"It was self-defense."

"Self-defense isn't premeditated. Wouldn't you say this is indicative of how you solve problems? Is that not what you did to the Waters family?"

"I don't know anyone with that last name."

The scene changed, morphed into the living room of Slim's house. He looked over to see nine year old Justin Waters perched on the edge of the couch. A greasy controller sat in his small hands. The kid's eyes were wide, but focused as he navigated his way through downtown Baghdad with an M-16.

"When do you think my parents are going to pick me up?"

Slim downed a chalky protein shake. Lenny and Wendy the Skank were supposedly on their way with the money and product they owed. Steroids weren't cheap and he explained the consequences of a fuck up like this when he agreed to sell to them.

"They should be here soon enough," Slim said.

"I'm hungry."

The voice from the interrogation room cut in. "Does this scene look familiar to you, Mr. Reuthe?

Slim didn't answer. He was mesmerized.

Slim went into the cramped kitchen, returned with some leftover tacos. Justin slid the waxy paper off them, took a bite, and then made a face.

"They're cold," he said.

"Ain't got a microwave. That's the best I can do."

Justin ate quietly.

Slim stood by the window overlooking the weed-tangled front lawn.

The scene kept unfolding.

It all went down as he remembered. Lenny banged on the door. Slim threw it open, ready to fight till he saw Wendy run up the driveway. The .38 in her hand winked in the moonlight. Slim slammed the door shut. Outside, the two lovers argued. Slim stormed into the room. Justin's eyes were wet.

"Are Mom and Dad mad at me?"

The Interrogator cut in. "It is in your best interests, Mr. Reuthe to tell us in your own words. A jury will be much more compassionate to someone who is remorseful about killing a child."

"I didn't kill any fucking kids," Slim said.

"That's not what your memory shows."

Slim grabbed Justin by his orange shirt collar, pulled him off the couch. Justin cried harder, fear filling tiny eye sockets. Two shots went off. Slim heard the sound of the door handle ring off the tile. He hefted the boy up to his chest.

"Hold on, Wendy! Jesus, he could have a gun!"

"Let me go! I want my baby back."

Slim had only meant to use the kid as a bargaining chip, not a shield.

Footsteps came in fast. Wendy ran into the room, gun out in front of her. The woman was barely twenty five, but looked forty with a three pack a day habit. She fired without thinking.

Blood dripped to the carpet in a soft pitter patter. The body in Slim's hands trembled. He let go. Justin crumpled to the floor, a ragged wheeze coming from his throat. The beige carpet turned dark brown.

Slim tried to close his eyes in the real world. It did him no good. The scene was still there. Slim watched as he knelt down and put his hand on the boys back. It rose and fell erratically and then stopped altogether.

When he looked up, Slim saw both Wendy and

Lenny's eyes turn cartoon-big. The gun fell from Wendy's limp hand. They just stood there, watching, waiting for Slim to act.

So he did.

Slim Reuthe broke every bone in Lenny and Wendy Waters' bodies. When it was finished, he picked up the gun, and put a bullet in each of their heads. Neighbors called the cops and by the time Slim was running through his backyard and hopping the fence, he could see red and blue lights bouncing off darkened windows.

"It was an accident. It wasn't supposed to go down like that."

"But it did. Do you know why a child lost his life in your home, Mr. Reuthe?"

Slim said nothing.

"Because you're toxic. This is what happens when people get involved with folks like you."

The electrodes pasted to his temples began to burn again. Sweat popped and dribbled. Bile crept up his throat, singing his oesophagus. The world turned into a grease smear and then his father's face came into view.

"Sometimes, Denny, bitches have to be taught a lesson. Otherwise, they walk all over you. That's the way of the world, son. It's one big fucking grinder. Don't be like me. Don't let it eat you alive."

"Can you tell me who this man is?"

"My father," Slim said.

In this scene a young Slim was seated at the kitchen table. He tried to stand up, but couldn't. The spoonful of cereal hung in his mouth, turned to mush. He wanted to help his mother. Every second she lay foetal on the dingy tile was a slice out of Young Slim's heart.

"Do you agree with your father's sentiment?"

"Sometimes. Depends."

"On what?"

The situation."

"Perhaps stealing a hefty supply of steroids and cash from you? Would that be grounds for teaching someone a lesson?"

"Don't know. I don't juice."

The machine dispensed a small piece of paper. On it was a list of drugs with a percentage next to them.

"Your toxicology report says different."

The memory continued on. Dad wrestled the chair away from Slim's mother, tossed it across the kitchen. It landed with a loud crash against the cabinet. Glasses and bowls rumbled.

"How many times do I have to fucking tell you, April? How many?!"

"I'm sorry, Beaux!"

Slim's mother covered her face. "Please, Denny, go watch cartoons."

"No," his father said. "He should watch. He needs to learn."

The vision cut out before the real beating began. Slim was grateful, but only for a second. Without warning the surrounding walls fell away like a box being opened by unseen hands. Slim looked down and the floor opened up and swallowed him.

It was a cycle, Slim realized. His parents had been fucked up and they, in turn, passed on the family tradition. Every deal he made; every jaw he broke; every acrid hit of speed or shot of steroids in a dingy backroom made him just like them. Slim wasn't blazing his own path; he was retreating his parent's steps. He wasn't getting away from their influence; he was nothing *but* the product of their influence.

Dad had died in a hospice, alone and angry. Slim never visited. Last he had heard his mother was living off SSI and mooching from the last remaining friends she hadn't alienated with her heroin habit—people sympathized until their shit went missing.

Which left Slim. The remaining Reuthe. A jobless fortysomething that camped out on an air mattress in an almost empty room rented out to him by one of the guys he worked the night-shift at a local grocery store before the higher ups had his ass booted for being *too* confrontational and aggressive toward the other employees.

It wasn't as if there hadn't been people that wanted to help, though. Plenty had tried to lift Slim out of his own pool of bullshit—especially Mariam, the only woman brave enough to stand up to the convict version of the Hulk.

When she agreed to take him in things were fine for a few months. He'd jog in the morning and attend night classes at Mesa College, chipping away at a GED.

It only lasted so long, though. Slim got bored fast. The monotony of a regular life grated on him. There was no stimulation; nothing to keep the demons at bay despite how much effort Mariam put into him.

One night, sitting on the balcony of her Lakeside apartment, Slim knew she was proud of him, but he still didn't feel proud of himself. He rolled a cigarette over and over between his fingers, contemplating if he should light it. What did it mean if he did? That he took a big leap backward, erased all the progress he'd made?

A cigarette wasn't steroids or crank, or a night of brawling, but even Slim knew that wasn't the point.

He remembered his Dad always told him that people had one angel and one demon on each shoulder. It was up to you to decide who led. Slim always felt like he'd gotten stuck with just a demon, as if God ran out of angels that day and said, "Well, they can't all be winners."

Only, the demon didn't sit on his shoulder clad in a black suit with one leg crossed over the opposite knee, like some stylish yuppie-type. No, Slim Reuthe's demon was an ugly thing covered in boils, riding him all the way down to the pit like a cursed jockey.

Another scene changed and the world shattered in front of him like a splintered windshield. In the shards he could see different moments of his life play out. He saw himself beat Kent Walwatne down outside Norma Jean's bar because Kent won a game of pool in front of a girl Slim wanted to impress—she left, disgusted by the macho act and Slim went home to jerk off.

There were more: His first steroid injection in the gym bathroom stall; Slim sitting on the lawn of his family's home, hands beat to shit after a fight with a neighbor. All of these memories bled together, ran over one another, like a big melting pot made out of every shitty decision Slim had ever made, until finally they formed a loose imitation of Slim's father's face.

"You are my son," said the abstract *dad face* in a sing song voice. "You always have been, you always will be, just a piece of shit like me."

The visage crumbled and Slim was back in the interrogation room. His hands shook. His mouth tasted of iron from gnawing his lip.

"This is who you are Denny "Slim" Reuthe. You've spent you're whole life running away from ending up like your folks, but the truth is, you've been winding that noose around your throat for a very, *very* long time."

"Fuck you. You don't know shit."

"Truth. Evidence. It doesn't lie. You've seen it right here."

Slim couldn't speak. Tears welled in his eyes. He felt microscopic. The muscles he had worked so hard to build became useless sandbags of flesh, hanging in his skin. They were useless here, proved nothing. The interrogator continued to hum, beep, and mock him over and over. It told Slim that he was just a statistic; a floating variable that could be traced back to a junkie mom and an alcoholic father.

Slim brought his forehead down on the metal table, screaming with each hit as the interrogator droned on.

Once.

"All you are…"

Twice.

"…is weak."

Three times.

"So admit what you've done."

The skin of Slim's forehead split. He kept his head down, grinding it into the table.

"I did it," Slim yelled. "I killed Lenny and his girl, but not the kid. I didn't…" His throat hitched. "…I didn't kill Justin."

"It was your actions that led to his death, though. And for what reason did this family suffer?"

"They ripped me off."

"Were you aware that Wendy was pregnant?"

"No," Slim said.

"The autopsy stated that she was a month into her term. Do you know what that means?"

Silence.

"Mr. Reuthe?"

"Yeah…yeah I fucking get it."

Slim sat up, eyed the smear of blood he'd left on the table.

The interrogator rose on a piston-like mechanism. Its belly opened and a small drawer slid out. On one side of the drawer there was a photograph; one Slim had seen only once.

It was one of the few occasions the Reuthe's tried to pretend they were a family, Slim's mother set them up with an appointment at a photo studio. In the picture their faces are strained, as if barbed wire clutched their bodies underneath the thrift shop dress clothes. No matter how hard Mom and Dad tried to craft some semblance of real home life, it always faltered, always broke under the weight of whom they really were.

They were a cancer to each other; and a cancer to their son.

The second section of the drawer held a grey pill.

"What now?"

"You have two options, Mr. Reuthe. Take the photograph and we send you back to your cell, but remember, Mr. Reuethe, prison isn't kind to child killers.

The Interrogator went on. "The pill, however, is a cure all. Swallow it up and you go away; we go away; the system doesn't have to waste another dime on a broken human being."

Slim stared at his only two options. All his life he'd just wanted to be respected. To not be treated like human garbage, so that he could feel something that wasn't hate or anger. The truth was, though, that in doing so, he'd only taken things from people—stolen lives in some cases. And in the end, it did nothing to salve the scars that burned Slim up day in and day out. No matter how much muscle he put on or skulls he cracked, inside he was still that frightened little kid at the breakfast table, hoping someone would save him.

The demon rode him hard and Slim could feel the flames fanning his face, as he reached out, and made a choice.

JUST FRIENDS

MICHAEL
W. CLARK

Despite his head pounding from being knocked unconscious and his arms being tied to the chair, Jake sat calmly. "Come on Tyler. I've known you all my life."

"I am younger than you." She held the crowbar as if it were a baseball bat.

"Oh, I can never get people's age right. I always think people are older than they are." Jake flexed his arms as far away from his body as he could. The chair creaked slightly.

"Not a very flattering thing to say to a woman." She swung the crow bar bat slowly.

"Age doesn't matter." Jake laughed.

"Don't say it's the mileage. That doesn't help."
She swung it very fast this time.

"Ah, well. I thought we were friends."

"You used to be fun when you were still drinking."
She moved her hands further up. She was choking the
crowbar bat. This swing was faster.

"Was I? I never remembered if I was fun or a
bore. Most drunks I meet are bores. Too caught up in
themselves to be interesting to anyone else." Jake flexed
his legs against the ropes. The wooden chair creaked
louder. "Thanks for being a fan."

"I wasn't a fan. I just said you were fun. Well
more fun than now. You being a cop an all." She stepped
toward Jake.

"I am a highway patrolman." Jake relaxed his
entire body.

"Still a cop." Tyler pulled back to get a full swing.

Jake flexed his leg abruptly causing the chair and
him to jump in the air. Jake leaned back slightly so the
chair came down on its legs at an angle. The legs broke.
Tyler screamed at the sound and motion. It made her
swing go wild.

Jake rolled toward Tyler and kicked her in the
chest with both his feet. She only grunted this time as
she sailed back into the concrete wall. Jake jumped to a

standing position. "You were right Tyler. We were never that close." He smacked the remains of the chair against the concrete wall until the wood was splinters and the ropes fell away. He did have to untie the ropes around his wrists. He watched Tyler while he did.

She was small but back in high school he had seen her get hit by a tree branch while she was standing up in a convertible. Jake had been driving. He wasn't going fast though, because he was driving drunk through a field. She was knocked out of the car into the field. She had gotten up and run after the car. She had seemed fine after that. Jake had been drinking from a bottle of cheap vodka the very instant she got hit by the branch. Was that what she meant by him being more fun while drinking? Maybe she would change her mind about him not being any fun now, since he just kicked her unconscious. "Now where did they put my stuff?"

His mother was calling him. He knew it was her because she had written a song and put it on his phone as her exclusive ringtone. He never knew how she got it on his phone though. Jake looked around the room he was in. It was a bunker left over from World War II and it smelled like it. The song was coming from a pile of trash in the far corner. "It must be lunch time. Mom always calls me at lunch time." Jake said to no one conscious.

Jake pulled his stuff off the top of the trash pile. His phone was in his hat. Thankfully and stupidly, his gun was still in its holster. He slung the holster over his shoulder and then answered his phone. "Hi mom."

"Why won't you have lunch with me?" She whined. Her voice was thick and slightly muffled.

"I do on the weekends." Jake looked over at Tyler. She was still crumpled against the wall.

"No! Not the weekend, Sunday. Just Sunday! Sunday's not enough." She slurred her words.

"It's more than enough." Jake muttered.

"What's tha' mean?" She sniffed. "I'm your mother."

"I know who you are, mom." Tyler was starting to twitch. "Mom. I am right in the middle of things."

"Your crime sluts are more interesting to you than me."

Jake rolled his eyes. "Don't drink so early in the morning. Especially with the medication."

"Know what I'm doing."

Jake didn't know whether that was a statement or question. "Got my job to do now."

"Eating lunch is important." She replied.

"Better than drinking it. Gotta go, mom." Jake clicked off.

Tyler sat up. She rubbed her chest. "Why'd you kick me?"

"You had me tied up and were going to hit me with that." Jake pointed at the crow bar beside her on the floor.

"You deserved it." She swallowed and coughed.

"Did not." Jake walked over and picked up the crowbar. "Second time someone knocked me on the head from behind. I didn't like it the first time either. I like it less now."

"Did not! If I'd done it, you wouldn't be here." She coughed again. "Think you broke a rib."

Jake patted his pants pockets. "My keys!" He looked out the open bunker door. Nothing was there but trees. He was only looking for his patrol car. He looked again. Still, nothing was there but trees. "Dammit, you stole my car too."

"I stole nothing. I'm right here." Tyler put her hands in the air. "You see a patrol car in here. A Fiat would barely fit in here. Jesus."

"What the hell's going on?" Jake put his holster back on around his waist. "Why were you going to bash me with this?" He bent down to pick up the crowbar and

Tyler jumped at him. Jake simply extended his arm and knocked Tyler back on to the ground. "What's with you? Attempted murder? Kidnapping? Interfering with an officer? Assault with a deadly weapon? I never thought you would graduate to felony criminal. What the hell happened? I thought, at most, maybe car theft. You could do that, but nothing felonyish." Jake nodded raising his eyebrows at her.

Tyler stared at Jake while trying to catch her breath. "We didn't steal your car." She coughed. "We just borrowed it."

"New definition of borrowing? Borrowing without asking is stealing, far as I know. Knocking someone out too doesn't fit with the standard definition either." Jake threw the crowbar over into the same corner where his stuff had been tossed.

"See! No fun at all." Tyler mocked. "You'll get the thing back. Just borrowed without asking because you became no fun at all."

"And a bash on the head? That punishment for my loss of entertainment value?" Jake rubbed the back of his head before putting on his hat.

"Stew did it. It wasn't me." Tyler pushed herself into a better sitting position.

Jake shook his head. "You were ready to prolong it

as I saw it."

Tyler shook her head. "You used to like it rough back in the day."

"You liked it rough. I didn't like feeling anything back then." Jake looked out the door again. Still, nothing but trees.

"I was supposed to just keep you here until they got back." Tyler gave a slight smile. "I was just threatening. I wasn't going to beat you up. Just putting on a show. You were the one hit me."

"Oh, so I'm the bad guy. So, this Stew? That's the Steward Prin from high school?"

Tyler increased her smile. "Jealous?"

"Of Stew? How could I be?" Jake took out his hand cuffs.

"That's why he hit you in the head. I told him not to." Tyler held her hands out like a Lady for Jake.

"Thanks for the support." Jake snapped the cuff on her scared wrists. "Done this before then? Tell me more. Or all of this will fall on your pretty little head."

"You think I'm pretty?"

Jake pushed Tyler over to another pile of trash and sat her down. She cooed as he did it. "A bit of advice, don't do crime while you're stoned. Just like driving. Don't do that either while high."

"You drove better out of your mind." She whispered.

"It's that tree branch. I knew it." Jake pointed at Tyler. "Stay!"

She replied. "Woof. Woof. Yes, Caesar."

"What could Stew want with a patrol car? It is meant to be conspicuous."

Tyler shook her head. "Need to know. I'm not a needy gal."

Jake stood to the side of the door frame. "A real free spirit, yeah." He scanned the old overgrown broken concrete road leading to the bunker. There were tire marks on it.

"I could float away sometimes." Tyler stated.

"You and my mother." Jake heard an engine in the distance. It wasn't his patrol car. He knew his machine's every sound.

"I liked your mother."

"Yeah, she's the life of the party." The engine sound got louder. An unknown car was coming this direction. Jake walked over to the pile of trash and retrieved the crowbar. "I'm going to barrow this for a few minutes." He held the crowbar toward Tyler. "See how borrowing works."

Tyler shrugged. "It's a cultural thing."

Jake laughed. "It is not." He got behind the door frame. "You keep quiet." He pointed at Tyler.

She shrugged again. "Is too."

Jake extended the baton he carried on his belt. "Quiet! Right?"

"Woof! Woof!" Tyler barked quietly.

Jake glanced out the door. The car was coming up the hill. He ducked back behind the frame.

The car pulled up. The engine revved and then shut off. Guys were laughing. Jake looked over at Tyler. He put his index finger over his lips for her to be silent. She blew a kiss back at him.

"Honey? We're home!" One of the guys called out. The other laughed.

As the first guy entered the door, Jake hooked his ankle with the bent end of the crowbar and flipped the guy on the ground. At the same time, Jake hit the second guy across the nose with the baton. Both guys yelled out on pain, simultaneously.

Jake kicked the first guy, who was face down on the concrete floor, in the coccyx. The guy screamed louder with the increase in pain. Jake hit the second guy in the throat with the baton and then grabbed him by the shirt throwing him on top of the first guy. Jake pushed the baton onto the back of the second guy's skull and searched for weapons. He found an automatic pistol and a hunting knife. He threw them into the trash pile. He searched the first guy too, finding two revolvers. They too ended up in the trash pile.

Jake rolled the top guy over. He pushed the bent end of the crowbar into the guy's sternum. He stepped on the back of the knee of the first guy who, despite being face down on to concrete, was still groaning loudly. "Hi Stew. Where's my car?"

"What the fuck!" Stew finally muttered.

"Yeah, what the fuck Stew?" Jake pushed the baton into the middle of Stew's back. "What did you do with my patrol car?"

"Tyler! You bitch!" Stew yelled.

"You Bastard! Back." Tyler replied.

"Answer me, Steward!" Jake stepped down harder on both guys.

"Hey, Stew answer him." Whined the second guy.

"Yeah, answer him Stewy. Also, where's the money?" Tyler laughed.

"You guys rob some place in my patrol car?" Jake pushed down harder. "Dammit. If there are bullet holes in it. I'll make some in you."

"No. No." Answered the second guy. "No one suspected the patrol car. No one followed. Stew was right."

Tyler laughed. "Surprises me!"

"Shut up, both ya!" Stew muttered.

Jake's phone rang. Thankfully, it wasn't his mother. It was the county sheriff. "Hello Sheriff."

"Jake, yeah. We found your vehicle. You weren't in it. Just thought I would call to see if you lost your hat again?"

"Oh thanks sheriff. No, no I have my hat. Thanks. I have three other things for ya though."

"Ya always givin' me presents Jake. I'm not your boss. Ha!"

"Well, I need a favor."

"Thought so. See what a detective I am. Deduce. Deduce. Deduce." The sheriff laughed loudly.

"Thanks Holmes. Could you bring my vehicle up to the old bunker on the point?" Jake stood up straight. His knee and back were complaining about his position.

"So that's where you runned off to. Funny place for a lunch time quickie." The sheriff thought himself very funny.

"Yeah, with my crime sluts, as my mother calls them." Jake laughed.

"Hey! Watch the name calling." Tyler whined.

"I'll be looking forward to seeing you then, sheriff."

Jake clicked off the phone and pulled out his service revolver. "You guys are going to stay right there but hug each other tight." Tyler laughed almost as loud as the sheriff had. "No, really! Hug each other tight. A big hug! Yes. Do it!"

"Those are my cuffs." Jake called out to the deputy putting Tyler in his back seat. "I'll pick them up later."

The Sheriff was standing behind Jake muttering. "I don't see it. Nope, but it must be there."

"What? Are you admiring my backside? Sexual harassment goes both ways." Jake chuckled.

"No, I can see that." The sheriff clapped Jake on the shoulder. "I was lookin' for the 'hit me in the head' sign. It's becomin' a regular thing with you." He laughed.

"Well, sheriff, at least, I get noticed."

The sheriff clapped him on the shoulder again. "What I went into law enforcement for too. Yeah. The attention. Ha!"

XIII

A BLUED ARMADA COMETH

GRAHAM WOODING

The gates to Swanforth mansion creaked in the slight gust coming from the ocean a short distance away. The rusted coating peeling to show pinkish rust, a sort of fleshy looking under side, it would remain pretty and ignored until exactly the time the world would end.

The path was of course overgrown, as were the bushes leading out from the gate pillars and around the housing property, its shambolic features suffering from perpetual morning hair. The Mansion itself was not quite so vagabond. White paint had been applied at great expense in the nineteen eighties when it was given title. A foreign ancestor of the man of the house had the same equally pompous title adorning his own residence. Industrial grade lacquer helped defend the brick and its crusting glue against the often whiplash wind seemingly thrown by the gulf. The remote location defended from the annoyance of lesser peoples.

The houses windows were greyed from years of filth and three were cracked from contact with Mrs. Herman's head whilst she was being brutally incapacitated in the kitchen. Byron looked up from his dominant position at her feet and over the brutalized body belonging to a ruler of nothing no more. He looked deep into her eyes, her head was caved in, three windows and a pick axe handle in the face tends to result in such atrocities.

Now for her legs.

The sadistic garden man looked along her slim body, a shiver had set in and her toes had curled up, a side effect of the massive unequivocal pain she now knew existed. He knew he was alone; a whole green swampy world lay between the house and other souls.

He twisted her legs until her whole body joined in and turned. Face down she could only whimper, her thoughts congregating in a miniscule part of her brain, the caved part of her skull was bruising by now and she could only hold her head up as the pain of contact with the floor bore a path to her inner sensors begging a furious NO!

He pulled her to the back of the house to an empty room once allotted the title of dining room. Here he broke her legs with the pick axe handle, an old foe in the employ of Mrs. Bitch's garden and now a new wooden friend for the fuming Byron. The screams were muffled; a silver spoon childhood was not good preparation for a triumph of wickedness, her mouth unable to take commands from her battered brain.

His mission, half complete would pause now and begin again in a jiffy as upstairs the man of the house was in the bathroom for what was to be his last shower. A cleansing for what he was about to receive, the gift of eternal hells. Suddenly the operatic music blasting from a bedroom stopped. A noise that masked the horror below cut off mid flow and the squeaks of a tap or two replaced it. Byron's ears on full power took all the sounds in.

Byron was a skilled man, a turbulent dalliance with his ground maintenance buddies and his newfound church of hidden sadism had left an indelible mark. He was surgical with his invisible theatre. He also saw the filthy cops at his church tent that day not long gone. They were cocky sniveling cunts, hiding behind sunglasses and shiny badges, eating the provisions provided by the lord for his flock, not two cheaply suited heathens gossiping like the unsullied girls they hunted for lust. Byron could smell them a mile off. Their sexual habits masked by the badged virtuousness of their chosen profession.

Byron had been considered slow in the eyes of the system and his filial overlords. He had however proven quick in the silent and dark arts of ritualistic murder. His daddy was too familiar and eventually too powerful, leaving the lonesome young Byron to his eventuality, a regime of cruel philosophy learned from the vulpine doings of false ecclesiastical abusers. Indelible atrocities lived everyday inside his skull and what was left of his heart. His was a cliché lot, obese and solitary he fitted the weird type exactly. But he didn't fit into it. It fitted into him.

Time was an irrelevance to the killer, he existed around times periphery and powers core, no old rich lady was going to ever bother him, but the enemy was passing by in their shiny machines.

And now for the husband.

He was to join his Ladyship in defeated stiffness then shit stained shrinking. Then a maggot festival would dance its evil dance, it must be evil, nothing else would dance at a time like this.

The pick axe handle was for fun, a twisted theatre

piece, earthly dalliance growing from boorish groundhog, the killer wanted what all god loving creatures wanted, freedom for their souls, and he would get his by balancing the brutal gifts of the good lord and wreaking vengeful campaigns on the Louisiana canvas with Satan's wrath. Evils terminal for the terminal human hid its self in amongst the folk living in its marshy organics and deaden trees and fields of feeble corn storks. Broken children littered the area. Victims were ten a penny and they would never speak of the times gone; Byron couldn't approach the reality of his. He could only share it, the burden too much, he must rid himself or worse things happen, his mind contracts and his blood moves in gulps. The headaches like the universe squeezing through his ears. Then comes the road trips and the digging and burning.

The blued armada continues.

Winning victory back from this family was not Byron's only goal. His sadistic yearnings born from the youth room with its black light graffiti and his lessons in how to pleasure god's messengers and circumnavigate reason, would become a reality at last, a last sonnet in this the very garden of his life's work. The lady of the house had basked in its glory unawares that he was building it for now not for her. His tenure of digging the precious grounds had afforded him the access he wanted, the immunity from guilt was a medal from the days of yonder. The daughter of the Herman couple was, is and had always been his passion. He would taste her blood then offering his dark master the rest of her, he would join the nether world a triumphant lunatic.

The double glass doors were open and the disabled pair of shivering tyrants lay on the floor heads turned to the world, a scream and thump from a bedroom. Then a limp body fell and thudded heavily on the patio. The daughter made no sound. Children should be seen and not heard. Even in the face of death she was a perfect daughter. Shock surging through the only energized part of the dying parent's fractured bodies, the eyes. All four widened, pupils shrinking into the future. The legs of the garden body moved. Then a hulking figure jumped down, landing awkwardly and nagging his leg, the slight on his macho image a fleeting issue as he was so close to the finale, just too lust fueled and semi-automatic. The parents would stare out at the flood lit garden, its expanse so big the night hid the boundary.

Again the Pickaxe handle.

The devil had done his dead. The stricken couples eyes watered and blinked, they could shut the quivering lids as much as possible, toes curled evermore they would suffocate looking at their hubris and their precious Edenish landscape draped in her blood, her lifeless body the centerpiece. Byron looked up and across the green. He had positioned the flood light to catch the drama and spill it daliesque on the garage wall with whitened fresh paint as per the plan. The shadows showing the two figures in flat blackened shape, then one shape grew horns and chants and howls, gouging true evil from its kraken depths. A short frisson of time would follow and see them through the welcoming parade.

The Blued light armada still cometh.

They were passing in the land bound distance in front the house, he knew only a matter of time before the devils came charging at him, hours, days, weeks, it could be a jazz trumpet solo of length. He would take his life before they took his freedom and answer the call to depart this broken world.

He wasn't sure the world had that many cars. Let alone in one place, he only knew the trucks of family members and walking. They seemed to Byron like flashing ants swarming a struggling fly. Byron didn't know the exact discovery those detectives made but he knew the occupants of the house for which the blued armada aimed, he knew them well. Whatever the reason the cops were magnetized, they were attracted to a piece of land down inland from the hill built colonial house of doom where Byron sat. The roads to the fly lit up like topographic veins.

Byron was watching from a porch in a chair rocking gently with victory. The chair had brought many bad times, as Mrs. Herman chose this antique piece to berate him in times of her loneliness. The family façade worked for those looking in but Byron had a close up and Mr. Herman was weak but cruel, a temper stemming from his lack of all else, Mrs. on the other hand was iron fisted and cold. Byron hated them for how they treated him and he hated them for how lonely and sad they made their daughter feel. Byron was not a man you want to be hated by. Now he was forced to bring the curtain down on his masterpiece early. The officers of whatever would find a monument to his existence in due course. He wanted it appreciated and poured over by the teams of scientist types who combed the crime scenes of the Yellow King.

And still Blue veins pulsated to the farm house.

His passion of grabbing victims and setting up kill rooms was over, no more could he exist; there was no point carrying on. He was ready for the ascension.

Before not long past, Byron had stalked the duo

in the church tent set up in a field. The minister gave a stirring delivery of Christ's work, a eulogy of Byron's inner most now's. His faith had been bound and sullied into serious darkness's, but Jesus kept him safe. The cops walked off to the quiet side to chat with some of the congregation. Pretty girls in dresses took a walk with the tedious looking of the pair. Byron had boiled his emotions in the bushes near and far from the strolling meat. Byron watched the girls humming their goodness's at the cop, he was shattered inside and confused deadly so.

The blued gets bluer still.

He did his kills up country; the detectives were on for a local killer. Byron pondered and chuckled at his lack of plurality. Many were dead by now, by many hands, the theatre at the house must have been spectacular like a twisted satanic circus from Paris or somewhere exotic.

Byron rocked the chair and guzzled whiskey, a bottle kept in the basement for special occasions and slipped into preacher mode. His mouth saying words itself, his eyes went back and back, white reddened balls replaced the norm. His chubby face wobbling, the sweat formed by lust only now dripping down his grayed face.

"Dark corners he knows your thoughts. The face

you wear is not your own, God knows I'm coming. God welcomes me."

Byron prayed for his soul and prayed for his arrival in the next kingdom. His work was not done yet; the lord was calling him for more.

"Don't let em divide you from what your heart knows."

The blued armada was thinning by now. All in the one place the flashing blue machines were stationary. The house that evil built was swarmed. The fly dead by now, Byron could only pray it suffered. His earthly torment bound by the deeds of the dwellers. Byron had snuck down not long ago. His body was trembling with the prospect of being caught. The fat mother of the house was tenacious in protecting the goings on. The beast would terrorize Byron's thoughts, every breath in was weighted by horror and every breath out congealed with toxic emotions. He had found a small outhouse with a chained human, so deteriorated he couldn't work out the gender. He ran. No matter how expert he was at his thing, he would never match the people and the house or the memories.

His end was nigh anyway, now more so the blued armada warmed up.

XIV

THE LORD PROVIDES

CHRISTOPHER
BROSNAHAN

Things happen to kids around this area. I went out onto the stage and gave the usual show. I made the blind see, the crippled walk and gave those with terminal cancer a clean bill of health. I laid hands on dozens of people and I walked away from that night with thousands of dollars.

I hadn't been around the Mississippi for a while. I'd avoided it.

Because every time I came here, I saw her again. At some point in the night, I'd lay my hands on someone, and when I lifted them again, I'd see her looking up at me, with that straw red hair around her face and those glassy blue eyes. I'd see her, and then I'd close my eyes for a second and she'd be gone and I'd know that it would take some extra liquor before I slept that night.

I thought back to when I'd started in this calling. This vocation. I thought back to Pastor Dean, my mentor, who I tried not to think of, but I always thought of when I was back in Louisiana.

I wish I could say that finding out that Pastor Dean liked to fuck little girls was the worst thing that happened. But lots of things happen to kids around here.

I'd started by helping film the shows. It was a summer job that my church had found for me, filming his sermons and helping out backstage. It was the day that he saw me singing with my guitar that he evidently saw something in me. I'd just been trying to impress some of the girls, but he saw enough showmanship that he took an interest.

He let me know that he saw big things for me. That the lord had told him I would be a big part of the church. And he convinced me to work full-time for them, rather than going back to my mom and dad.

He then had me working as one of his personal assistants. This meant bringing the items people weren't meant to know about from venue to venue - the wheelchairs and canes, which we'd convince people to use to give the illusion that they were sicker than they were, before they were dramatically hurled aside.

It also meant making sure nobody was around when he was with the girls, who he'd take back to his private sanctum under the story that he was providing a personal healing. I'd stay outside, and officially, I didn't know what was happening, although the other assistants talked. He preferred them younger, and he explained to me why one night when he was drunk.

"They don't tell anyone, Nicky," he said. "Kids like that, they're brought up to do what they're told. The younger you get them, the more scared they are of what will happen to them, the better they behave."

Lilly Wilson was eight years old. Just the right age for the pastor. The right age to do what she was told and still be able to be scared of talking.

He'd done this plenty. All over the country.

This time though, after a while, he came out.

He asked "Do you love the lord and love me?"

I said yes.

He opened the door and brought me in.

Lilly Wilson was lying dead on the floor, her eyes looking upwards. Her skirt was hiked up and her ripped underwear was lying next to her. There were thick red marks around her neck.

I don't know why I reacted so calmly, but I did. "What do you need me to do, Pastor Dean?" I asked.

He put his hand on my shoulder from behind. "The lord has sent you to help me," he said. "Thank you for being the lord's servant."

A week later, he involved me on stage for the first time. Holding his props and reading bible verses for him. When I finished that night, he walked me into his private room, which was richly decorated.

He pointed to the marble table. There was an envelope with my name on it.

"What's this?" I asked.

"Your cut for tonight," Pastor Dean said, pouring a glass of bourbon. "You've earned it, son."

There was more money than I had ever seen before. Most of it in fives and ones, but there were twenties and fifties there. Even hundreds.

Pastor Dean smiled, sipping his drink. "It's something, ain't it?"

"I just..." I stumbled over my words. "I had no idea."

"Doesn't get taxed either," he said, putting the

glass back down and settling back into his chair. "We're a religious institution. God bless the separation of church and state."

"But you have to declare it?" I said. "Even just the administration of it all..."

He laughed. "Only as much as we want and only if we want. The money's ours. You do as well as I think you can do, boy, you'll be a millionaire before you're 25. I'll teach you to do as I do."

I looked at the notes. Not for the first time, I thought about the people who had given it. The desperate. The needy. The ill. They dying.

"You ever..." I kept looking at the money. "You ever feel bad about this?"

He got up and walked across to me, looking directly at me until I couldn't bear it anymore and looked back. "What do we have to feel bad about, Nicky?" He asked.

"Well, there's - I mean, there's... you know, people giving the last of their money and all." I struggled to keep his gaze, but I did.

"And what does that money buy them?"

It buys them a subscription to begging letters and occasional trinkets, I thought, but didn't say. "It - it buys them..."

"It buys them hope, son. It buys them faith. It buys them a belief in God. When we go out there and we tell our little stories to make them believe in us, they believe in the lord more."

I nodded. "I understand." I clutched the envelope.

He sighed and put his hand on my shoulder. "We have been given a burden, son. We've been asked to perform these little stories, but we don't do them for personal gain. I could never be a liar, and God knows that. But I can tell stories. I can make people believe more."

I nodded and I thought about the week before.

We'd wrapped Lilly's body in an altar cloth and carried her to the back of my car.
We took the spare tire out of the trunk and laid her down, still wrapped in the cloth. And then I drove with the Pastor in the passenger seat, directing me.

We came to the crematorium where he directed me round to the back of the building. There were high walls on all sides, and the only other car looked like it had been there for a long time.

Then we went into the main entrance, where the Pastor spoke to the funeral director, who brought us into the back, where the caskets were kept before the incineration, so he could pray over them.

After a little further discussion, the director pointed towards a particular casket, which was on the trolley.

It was a closed casket, due to the injuries sustained in the car accident. There was no way that anybody wanted to look at the remains of what had been a drunk driver once he'd gone through the glass that tore his face to shreds and been propelled into the side of the truck. There was just too much of his face and chest missing.

The director left us alone to pray for a few minutes.

"The lord has sent this man for us." Pastor Dean said. "I'll take the funeral director aside for a while, to go through the funeral arrangements."

I looked at the casket, which seemed to take up the whole of my vision for a moment, before blinking and looking back at him. "And what do you want me to do?" His eyes lit with irritation. "What the fuck do you think I want you to do, boy? Get the child and put her into the casket. Then close it again."

My stomach churned. "What?"

"The car is round the back, and you can come in here through that —"

He pointed to the small door behind me. "—door there, while I keep the director busy."

I looked at the door and didn't say anything,

although I wondered how well he knew what to do.

"The lord be with you," he said as he left to talk to the director.

I stood there. Briefly, and for the only time in my life, I thought about running. About calling the police. But I thought of the lord.

And I opened the casket.

The man inside was a mess. Half of the skin on the left side of his face was missing and a large section of his skull was caved in. His eye was missing, and in the years since that night, that's been the image that my brain has retained.

I then opened the door and went to the car. I opened the trunk of the car. She was still there. Of course she was.

Gently, I lifted her out of the trunk. She was lighter than I expected. I held her close to me as I rushed back into the crematorium. I could feel some of the cold skin of her face against my neck.

I was frightened by the time I was back at the casket, but managed not to panic as I removed the altar cloth.

I shifted her weight and looked at the casket, working out where I could lay her. Lifting her into it was difficult, and I worried about knocking over the casket. But

I was careful and I managed to do it.

I laid her across him, her head against his shoulder. Her body against his, her arms slumping down at his sides. An embrace.

That morning, when the cremation took place, I watched the casket move slowly into the covered area. I didn't see the flames reducing them to ash, but I imagined it. I imagined her glassy eyes as the flames came closer.

As I write this, the bottle of liquor is half empty.

I tried to sleep, but I saw her again. Memory is the real burden.

I have more helpers now than Pastor Dean ever did. They go out for me during the start of the show and talk to people. The thousands of people that come to the shows every week that get added to the mailing lists.

We don't use email. Letters work so much better. The old-fashioned approach. The personal touch. The little gifts we put in with them that cost us dollars, and then the envelopes we include requesting them to send money back.

They fall over themselves to do it.

And when my helpers go out and talk to people, they can't wait to tell them everything about what's wrong with them, so when I go out later, I just call on them and tell them all that information right back, and they believe the lord did it.

The burden I take on to help them believe. The stories I weave and the lies I tell.

And the secrets I keep.

Months later, I sat in the church while Lilly Wilson's parents looked at us with hurt in their eyes—that hurt pushing outwards with stinging redness.

"We just want to know what happened, Pastor. Want you to ask God, ask Jesus for us. What happened to our girl?"

The tears ran down her father's face as he asked. I wanted so much to be able to make him feel better. To tell him that God loved him, even if I couldn't tell him anything else.

I leaned forward and took his hand. "I'll pray for you," I said.

"Don't give them false hope," Pastor Dean said. "I abhor giving people false hope."

I let go of her father's hand, and looked at him, surprised.

"Michael, I..." he sat down next to me, his voice

soft, "I'm sorry, but I spoke to the lord last night for you, I spoke to the lord Jesus, and I asked him already for you. I couldn't have lived with myself if I hadn't, but what the lord Jesus told me, I'm sorry."

He'd started using the same manner and style of speech that he used when he was performing on stage.

"I couldn't see that little girl... that beautiful little girl... go missing and not try to do whatever I could, use whatever ability Jesus gave me, to try to find her for you, Michael.

Her mother hugged her father, who wept into her shoulder.

"So I spoke to the lord for you, Michael and Janet. I spoke to the lord. And I asked him what had happened to your beautiful girl. And he told me - and I wish I didn't have to tell you this, I really do, but I made a promise to the lord - that... that..."

As on stage, that moment of hesitation. The reminder that he was just a man, trying to do God's work.

"...that God took her away to punish you. To punish you for your wicked ways, and I won't tell either of you what God told me about the other, but you both know that you've done wicked things over the years."

They both looked at him, the grief and anger palpable. He continued.

"You haven't prayed enough. You haven't given enough when we've been collecting, you haven't believed in your hearts enough. And the lord took her away to make an example out of you."

"You can't say that," her mother said in a low growl.

"I'm not saying it, Janet. The lord is saying it, and you know in your hearts that it's true."

"We loved her!" she shouted. The silence hung in the air. I had no idea what to say.

"Well, now, that's the problem, isn't it?" the Pastor said. "You loved her, but it should have been God that you loved first. It should have been the lord that you loved most, because he loved her, and he took her back. She's in heaven at the lord's side."

"She... she's dead?" her father said. He gripped his wife. "The lord told you she's dead?"

He ignored the question and raised his voice as he talked. "You putting your needs ahead of God's needs, your love ahead of God's love, your wants ahead of God's wants?"

"We never - " her mother said, the upset catching in her throat.

"That is Satan's work!" the pastor cried. "Satan's work, that had your child taken away from you! Satan that drove you to have less faith than you needed! Satan and the devils that drove the wickedness in your hearts that led you to this!"

"Please," her father said, letting go of his wife and falling to his knees. "Help us. Help us love God and get our daughter back."

"I cannot help you," he said grandly, standing up. "Go back home and pray. The lord is angry with you. That is why this has happened. Go back home and pray and beg for forgiveness. It's too late for me to help you now. You should have come to me sooner, instead of going to the police. You were arrogant and you were foolish and you were evil. Go back home and pray."

"Please," her father said again, clutching at his wife and trying to pull her to her knees next to him. "I know we've been wicked. I know we've been out of God's favor. But please, just help us pray to the lord now, if nothing else."

He looked down at both of them, the father kneeling and the mother sitting. "I cannot do that, Michael. It would make a liar of me to beg the lord to do differently than he has done, and I cannot condone that request." He pointed to the door. "You should leave my church now, the two of you. Leave and do not come back. This is a house of the lord."

There were more tears, and more upset, but there were no more words. The father left, pulling the mother with him. She had more fight in her, more anger in her, but the bruises on her wrist said that she was used to punishment.

The pastor looked silently at the door for a while.

"What do you think they'll do?" I asked.

"The lord will guide them," he said. "They won't make any trouble."

He was wrong, but only just. There was a little more trouble. The Wilsons died that night, after the father strangled the mother and then hanged himself.

I don't know what happened between them, but I have a pretty good guess. My reckoning is that she threatened to go to the police again, and he killed her. Then, filled with grief through the loss of his wife and daughter, he killed himself.

When I told the pastor was told that the police had decided Lilly's father had probably killed her too, he chuckled. "I told you, Nicky," he said. "The lord provides."

That was forty years ago now, and Pastor Dean is long dead. He died peacefully, surrounded by the luxury that the lord's work had afforded him.

And I have grown rich through my ministry. Through my healing. And through the lord's good will.

While I see her face sometimes, in my mind, it doesn't matter. Not in the big scheme of things.

Secrets stay kept in Louisiana.

walk hand in hand into extinction

XV

"A clear conscience is the sure sign of a bad memory."
- Mark Twain

Los Angeles – 7/14/1997

When Detective Zamora walked inside of her office, she found that Detective Brett Hunt was already there. The room smelled different than usual. And Hunt looked different, too. His cheekbones seemed more prominent than ever and his eyes were bloodshot.

The table was full of dossiers of old cases they had worked on in the past.

-What are you doing here? I'm always the first to get here. –she said.

He did not answer and, instead, rubbed his eyes.

-Wait, did you sleep here? –she asked.

-Technically I *stayed* here. I haven't been able to sleep a wink. —he said, his voice rough.

-I think you need a break. A vacation would be good for you. —Zamora suggested.

-What makes you be you? —Hunt asked her, ignoring the last comment.

-What?

-Is it your face? Is it your voice? —he said. She had no idea what was going on.

—No. It's the memories. Without them, you're nothing. A hollow entity. The sum of all your experiences, that's what makes you who you are.

-I don't get it. —she said, speaking candidly.

-Do you believe in ghosts? —Hunt said.

-Ghosts? As in poltergeists? Like a girl wearing white on the side of the road? No, I don't.

-No, I mean like *real* ghosts. Memories that will come back to haunt you. —He stopped and took a deep breath.

— I don't want to wake up in the middle of the night seeing her. I don't want her telling me that she was innocent and feeling responsible for her death, because I didn't do enough. I've been checking old cases 'cause I was afraid that we could have sent an innocent person to the gas chamber...

Zamora didn't know what to say. She had never seen him

like this.

-What happened to you? What's all this about?

Hunt hesitated.

-I visited her. -he said.

-When?

-Yesterday.

Los Angeles – 7/13/1997

Detective Hunt had been waiting in the visitation area
of a women's prison somewhere near a California desert.
He was standing in front of a glass window, awaiting her
appearance.

A girl walked in and sat on the other side of the glass. She
was wearing an orange jumpsuit.

Hunt picked up the phone, and so did she.

-Hi, Audrey. How have you been? –Hunt said.

-Fine, I guess. –she answered.

-Sorry I haven't been here in some time. I've done my best
but I haven't found anything new.

-I've got three months. –Audrey said, cold. –My execution
date is the eleventh of September.

Hunt did not respond.

-I've been reading a lot lately, you know? –She said- I
followed your recommendations, actually.

-And what have you been reading?

-Nietzsche, Sate.

-Sartre. —he corrected her.

-Yes Sartre. And some more. The other day I came across a sentence… It's been stuck in my head. *"Some men are born posthumously."* —she said.

-Nietzsche. From *The Anti-Christ,* right?

She nodded her head.

-What about it? —he asked.

-I was thinking that he was right. I was thinking that I have no memories prior to that day we met at the hospital. So whoever I was—that person is dead. And whoever I am now, whether I am the same person, or a different one, I'll die for a crime that I don't know if I committed. In some way, I was born posthumously.

Once again, Hunt kept quiet. There was not a word in the English language that he could use to comfort her. She looked so sad, lost, and resigned.

Hunt instinctively put his palm to the glass, trying to reach her hand.

-I promise I'll do everything in my power to help you. —he said.

-I read Sartre's *No Exit,* too. —she said, ignoring him.

Hunt did not answer.

-He was wrong, you know.

-Wrong about what? -Hunt asked.

-"Hell is other people" —she said. -Hell is not other people.
Hell is when you're left alone with your own thoughts.
Hunt sat there silent, contemplating her words. He was
about to say something, but Audrey spoke first.

-Some days I wish I could remember—just so I could
prove myself innocent. And some days I'm glad I can't.
Because I'm afraid to wake up and see my hands covered
in bloodstains. —she said.

Audrey hung up the phone and left the room.

Los Angeles – 7/14/1997

Zamora had been listening to his story for over six minutes
now. Being a bit of a sceptic, she struggled to avoid
interrupting him every couple of seconds. Finally, when
Hunt did finish, Zamora said -Don't you get it? She's been
playing with your head. She's trying to brainwash you.

-No. You know that I have a gift for reading people and
I'm telling you, she's not lying. I could see the truth in her
eyes.

-Try explaining that to the judge. "Hey, she's innocent—
trust me. Just take a look at her eyes." I'm sure you'll be
very convincing... —Zamora smirked at him smugly. -We
work with facts, Hunt. That's what we do. We *prove* things.

And the only way to do that is with *physical* evidence.

As much as he hated to admit it, Zamora was right. There was no way to prove her innocence based on a look.

-Are you going to help me with this or not? –he said.

She remained silent some time before answering.

-Before I accept or decline your offer to work on this case *in my free time*, because—let's be honest—the boss won't approve of this, I need to know something.

-What?

-I want to know what the point of this is.

-What do you mean?

-Are we doing this to save her, or are we doing this for justice?

-What are you suggesting? –he asked.

-I want to make sure that whatever the result of this investigation is that we'll go all the way with it. Even if it proves completely opposite to whatever theory you may have right now.

-Yes, that is the point. I want to find out what happened. If she did it, I want to prove it. If she's innocent I want to prove that as well. –Hunt said.

-All right. When do we start then?

-Tomorrow. 7:00 A.M. at my place. Don't be late. –said Hunt as he left the room.

Los Angeles – 8/27/1997

Zamora knocked at the door twice. She was on Hunt's porch. They had been working on the case for over a month and a half and still had yet to prove whether or not the girl, Audrey, was innocent or guilty.
Nobody opened the door but she had heard her partner speaking from inside the house.
Hunt said -Come in, the doors' unlocked. –So she did.
Brett was seated in a chair at the center of his living room. It had served as a personal office since the investigation began. All over the walls and floor of the room were strings that connected to post-its and written events on note cards. Zamora thought that given a different set of circumstances, this could all be considered artistic—but she didn't comment.
Brett stared at her.
-I don't know where else to go with this. –he said.
-We must be missing something. Let's go over it again...
Seeing Zamora invested, to some extent, gave him a boost of confidence. He got up and grabbed a couple of dossiers.
-The victim –he said. –Douglas Bennett. Thirty-one years old. Son to Raymond Bennett, the famous movie producer. Cause of death...

-Stabbed seven times with an unknown weapon… Twice in the stomach, three times in the chest, once in his left arm and ribs. –Zamora said. –A man, Robert Carter, found them unresponsive not far from the Hollywood Art Institute.

-The suspect –Zamora said. -Audrey Sophie Miller, 19 years old. It says she was studying acting. No known family… No phone… Claims to have amnesia and doesn't remember anything prior to waking up in the hospital.

-She studied at the Hollywood Art Institute. First year student. Found unconscious next to Bennett with a severe head wound. –Hunt said, almost reciting the words.

-Weapon?

-A Bowie knife—which has yet to be found.

A big silence occupied the room.

-We've got nothing. –Zamora said. –Nothing useful.

-We need to dig deeper.

-Deeper? If we dig any more we're gonna pop up in China.

Hunt did not respond. He felt empty, as if he had given everything he had and come up short.

-We could always… Falsify some proofs… –Zamora suggested, her voice timid.

Brett looked at her.

-Just to get her a prorogation, and to give us some more

time. –Zamora said.

-I don't like your methods. –He said, staring at her.

-I don't give a shit. –She said. –I'm just trying to help.

Hunt said nothing.

-The end justifies the means, you know?

-Machiavelli. –Hunt said.

-What's Machiavelli? –She asked.

-A kind of Italian food. I'm hungry -he said, rolling his eyes in despair. Hunt was surprised that she didn't know the person she had just quoted, but was even more surprised that she didn't know that Machiavelli was a person.

-Good idea. Let's get some Italian food. I'm hungry, too.

They were back at Hunt's home eating some pasta from an Italian take-away restaurant, reading their notes over and *over* again.

-Why are we doing this? –Zamora asked, frustrated to no end. Her hair was frazzled, and her mind was a fog of emotion. –How is this case any different than the others we've worked on?

Hunt thought about that.

-I don't know. It surprised me that everything went so fast... –he said. –Three weeks after we found Bennett dead,

Audrey was already behind bars with a death sentence under her arm. If that's not unusual, I don't know what is.

-What do we know about the victim? Other than where he came from and who his father is?

-Let me look into it.

Zamora started reading through papers and notes and dossiers. Trying to find anything related to the victim, Doug Bennett.

-Here… –she said showing him a small dossier. –This is interesting.

Brett started reading it.

-Two accusations of sexual assault. –He read aloud.

-But no charges were ultimately filed. –Zamora said.

Hunt sat there, mulling it over.

-I have a theory. –He said.

-Please, expand upon it. I love to hear you ramble.

–Zamora said, her voice dripping with sarcasm.

-Like I said, it all went too fast.

-Yeah, and?

-Not only did it go fast, but we were pushed out of the case two days after we talked to the victim's father.

-Because we were moved to a more important one…

-Yes, but the case fell in the hands of Dobbs who, for all intents and purposes, is probably the most inept person ever employed by the L.A.P.D.

-But—

-Who also happens to be driving an Aston Martin —he interrupted her. —A car that costs around $200,000. A car that he got one week after he was assigned that case. —He stopped to loosen his tie. —I've been working in this field for more than thirty years and I can't even afford a fucking bike.

-Are you suggesting that his father is bribing people to get the girl sentenced to death?

-I'm not suggesting it, I'm saying it. As much as I like his movies, I think his dad moves more strings than a fucking puppeteer. In this town, he has fingers longer than an octopus' tentacles.

Zamora sat, unresponsive.

-*"One must not let oneself be misled: they say "Judge not!" but they send to Hell everyone and everything that stands in their way."* —recited Hunt.

-Who said that? – Asked Zamora.

-Nietzsche did.

-And who's that?

Again, Hunt was amazed by her ignorance.

-A comedian —he answered, smiling.

-So he's doing all of this to avenge his son? —Zamora said, puzzled.

-Maybe not to avenge his son. Maybe only to silence her.

Maybe he wants her executed before she can remember something.

-I'm not sure what to think… But that almost makes sense.

-Go back to the office. Bring everything you find about Doug Bennett and the victims of those two sexual assaults.

Zamora, wasting no time, rushed out and went directly to the office.

…

The phone next to Hunt rang. He picked it up.

-Yes?

Zamora was on the other side.

-Brett, I may have found something.

Los Angeles – 9/11/1997

Hunt was standing in front of the Judge; waiting for him to finish reading the dossier he had just given him.

He tried to hide how nervous he was because he knew time wasn't playing in his favor.

The judge read everything slow and carefully.

He knew all the hard work; all the days sleeping less than three hours had led him there. Two months of hard work.

Working on his free time, digging as deep as he could to find out what had really happened… And he did. He could prove them wrong. He could save her. He now had facts, not theories.

-Do you support this? –The judge asked.

-I do. –Hunt answered, firm in his conviction.

The judge signed the papers that Hunt had given him and then handed them back.

-Thanks –Hunt said, as he grabbed the dossier and left running.

He got inside the car that was parked outside. Zamora was sitting behind the wheel.

-Hit it – Hunt said.

Zamora was on the wheel, driving and Hunt, as usual, was sitting next to her, looking outside of the car.

-God, I hate this town. –He said- the whole world knows it for its glamour and fame, but they're blind to the filth. In order for a few to live the good life they need a whole bigger bunch to live in the dirt. –He stopped to take a breath. -All these youngsters who come here looking for fame and money think this city is special and that it'll help them get to the top, but that's bullshit. The media only tells you about the ones who survived. They know nothing about those who ended up lost and rotting in the crevices of this town.

-I don't even know what the fuck you're talking about, Brett. -Zamora said.

Hunt shook his head. He kept checking the clock every

now and then, nervous.

They stopped in front of the prison where Audrey was set to be executed. Hunt had been told that a call would be made to pardon her. But with so many crooked enforcers in the city, he *needed* to know that she'd be safe. That her life would be spared.

Once they arrived, Hunt hopped out of the car. He raced toward the prison as fast he could. For a fifty-one-year-old man his speed was impressive.

Raymond Bennett, the father of Doug Bennett, as well as some others, were seated in front of a one-way mirror. On the other side was Audrey Miller, tied to a bed, about to be injected with the mix of sodium thiopental, pancuronium bromide, and potassium chloride.

This was his idea of justice. An eye for an eye.

Less than three minutes away from seeing his son avenged, Raymond noticed, through the glass, that one of the guards looked agitated—confused.

The door of the room opened and Detective Hunt walked inside. He handed some papers to the guards and then left. After reading them, they carefully proceeded to untie the girl from the bed and escorted her outside of the room. The governor's office wouldn't call the prison for another six minutes, with the same exact information.

Raymond Bennett stormed out of the room in a fury, only to find himself facing Detective Hunt.

-What do you think you're doing? —Raymond asked and saw the girl leaving the room with two guards.

-Murderer... —He screamed at her. Audrey stared at him, afraid. But Hunt shoved him away.

-Leave her alone, she's innocent.

-She killed my son... —Raymond said, and pushed him back. Hunt almost toppled over, but regained his balance. In return he struck Bennett once across the face.

Bennett collapsed, his nose pouring blood.

Two men rushed to help him up.

-This is unbelievable... —Bennett whined.

-Make a movie about it. —Hunt said, and walked away.

Zamora's car stopped at the front of a dingy, little house. They were in a small neighborhood in Los Angeles. Hunt turned to the backseat, where Audrey was sitting.

-This is yours. —he said.

-Is it?

He handed her the keys that had been kept in custody since she had been detained.

-Fancy a coffee? If there's any. —she offered the two.

-I don't think it'd be ethical. –Hunt said.

-Please. To thank you for saving me.

-Okay. One cup. –he said.

-Thanks, but I'll wait out here. –Zamora said.

They exited the car and walked to her house.

Inside there was dust everywhere. It hadn't been cleaned in several months.

Hunt was standing in the middle of a living room holding a cup of coffee in his hands. Audrey was looking for something to eat.

He felt as if he was drinking a bottle of champagne after winning the 24 hours of Le Mans. That coffee was like heaven to him, even though it lacked any kind of quality taste. It was the reward for all the hard work he had put in; the lack of sleep and endless days had not been in vain.

-Damn Audrey, that's some good coffee. Best I've had in a while. –He said –By the way, where's the bathroom? –he asked, off-handedly.

-Upstairs, second door to the left –Audrey responded without hesitation.

They were both paralyzed, aware of what had just happened.

The sound of a shattering cup, falling to the floor, broke the silence between them. A silence that seemed eternal to her.

DEFILEMENT

GEORGE
P. FARRELL

The cinder road came out of the darkness and continued on into the darkness. Its soft banks sloped steeply down to the marshes on either side. There were no stars in the sky that the boy could see. He couldn't even see the marsh grasses and cattails he knew were down there on either side of the road. The only light was from the glowing coals of the dying fire. He was surrounded by darkness and did not want to get close to the embers that shimmered orange in the center of the deserted cinder road. He did not want to see what remained within the glowing embers. The boy turned in slow circles looking for movement. Sensing something, out there in the darkness, but it wasn't moving now. Not yet anyway. The boy crept closer to the warm embers. He wanted to see, and yet he didn't want to see what the fire had done. He feared looking into the fire. He feared seeing what had turned to white ash and now lay inert. And he didn't want to be seen. He felt utterly lost.

He dared not walk down the cinder road in either direction. And sliding and slipping down the soft embankments would bring him into the mire of the marshes. Why were there no stars, nothing to provide guidance? No melodic voice from his mother calling to him, giving direction. Come here, this way. The boy's breath constricted in his chest till it felt like a balled fist struggling to get out. Then the movement. At first he thought he imagined it. It was on the other side of the fire. As it approached, the orange embers outlined the black, looming form. The boy backed away, his movements deliberate, dreamily slow, till he was at the edge of the cinder road. The shadowy figure was blotting out the embers and the white ash. It was on his side of the fire now and approaching. It had seen him. It moved quickly toward him. The boy scrambled over the edge of the road, through the deep, loose cinders that sloped steeply downward. He lost his balance and tumbled head over heels crashing to the bottom and rolling into the deep weeds, the ground here boggy, sticky, and malodorous.

The dark shape was loping down the slope after him. The boy got up and ran into the tall reeds, the hard stalks slapping at him, the muck pulling at his feet, his heart racing, pounding, the sweat pouring from his face…

… Dick Hennessy sat bolt upright in his bed, swung his legs and feet to the floor and stood up in one spastic motion. He was bathed in sweat, his heart pounding. He hated that cinder road. It wasn't the road less travelled. It was the road never travelled. By anyone. But it kept coming back. Again and again. There he'd be on the cinder road with the dying embers and the dead white ash and the ultimate approaching darkness.

Lemke said, "The deer was gut shot. If you don't bleed it out fast, the meat all tastes like liver."

The two men stared at the carcass of the whitetail deer airing out inside the bleeding-room, off to one side of the kitchen, Olga out there somewhere battling with pots and pans. They sat at a scarred butcher block table and stared through the opening in the wall to where the deer hung from its hind end dripping blood through a hole in the floor. The blood pooling in the swampy muck under the old clubhouse.

When January arrived they all sat around the table, Lemke and Captain Hoke smoking cigars, January wishing she had a butt. The summery air drifting in through a screen door had the salty smell of the surrounding wetlands.

"Venison. For the Fourth," Lemke said, gesturing toward the deer.

January glanced at the animal then turned back to Lemke. She said, "You wanted to see me about something?"

"I don't want to hear your thoughts. I just want you to think them."

"What am I supposed to think?"

"That could be you hanging in there. Airing out so to speak."

January glanced at the gutted, decapitated deer. "The deer's out of season. What's your point?"

Olga in the kitchen, all three hundred pounds of her, bustling about, now using the meat cleaver on something. Chop. Chop. Chop. January thinking this is theatre.

She said, "You might want to try this out in New Haven. I don't think it's ready for Broadway."

Captain Hoke pulled his chair close to hers, filled her view with his large, craggy face, not a hint of kindness in it, the man spending most of his adult life crafting that look.

"Listen, Sweetheart. Any day now we could pay you off, put you in a limo and send you off to California where you can pursue a career in the movies."

"Like the other girls who disappeared, huh?"

"That's right. There's quite a few out there in Hollywood. Trading blow jobs for bit parts."

"You ought to visit me once in a while, Hoke. Loosen up your tight ass. That is if you can get it up, which I doubt."

Hoke launched a stiff right hand knocking the girl over backwards in her chair. Creating a wooziness inside her head, her thoughts jumbled. But she forced herself to get up, straightened her chair, sat back down and smoothed her dark hair in place. Nothing to it.

"You're a manly man, aren't you," she said.

Hoke's face steaming. Lemke held up a restraining hand. There was no point in permanently damaging the girl. They still needed her.

Lemke blew smoke in the direction of the whitetail. "Get Dick on board."

"Onboard? I don't know what you're talking about."

"January, don't bullshit me. You know what's going

on here. Dick needs to marry Melissa, even if it only lasts a few months."

"They're first cousins, for Christ sake."

"I don't care they're brother and sister. He won't listen to me, but he's nuts about you. Convince him it's only temporary. Tell him, he does this, he'll never have to work another day in his life. Tell him you need him to do this."

Silence.

Lemke said, "Get it done and life can be sweet, real sweet. Don't and you could be hanging in that closet waiting for Olga."

Olga's meat cleaver whacking away at something that used to be alive and well.

January stopped in front of the door. The brass sign read Dill Docks Club, Manager. She knocked. Dick Hennessey let her in.

"There's something strange going on," she said.

"Strange," Dick laughed. "That's an understatement."

"I'm not talking about Melissa and Old Jake," she said. "Something else, I can't put my finger on. But maybe there's a connection."

"Like what?"

She said, "You've been in Lemke's office downtown?"

"A few times," said Dick.

"You know the layout?"

"It's a suite of individual offices. Lemke's got the corner one. The big shot office. River view."

"Dick, Bob Moses is going to build a bridge here. Before it's built, it needs roads leading to it. That means purchasing land, lots of it. Swamp land. Worthless at the moment. But could become very valuable. Particularly if Old Jake has his way with Melissa; he swings a deal through Shannahan and the Board of Estimate. The price gets jacked. There's a lot of money at stake."

"Jake's not getting Melissa. I won't let it happen. For Christ sakes, the Bronx is not the fuckin' Fiji Islands."

"Who owns that land, Dick? All that swamp land from Throgs Neck to Pelham Park?"

"Flattop. Up until he died."

"Who're Flattop's heirs?"

"He had no children."

"How do you know?"

"I never heard of any."

"I have a friend used to be in the business," said January. "She got a dose once too often and went for a real job. She cleans offices in the Empire State building."

"What are you saying?"

"We go in there, dress like the cleaning crew. Take a look at his files. I want to see Flattop's will."

"These guys can play rough."

"Dick, if they're into eating the occasional nubile female, how much rougher can they get?"

"Jan, this is an eating club, not a cannibal club. We don't eat people here."

Silence.

Dick hesitated, weighing consequences against possible gains. "When you want to do it?"

"Tonight."

"What's the rush?"

"My life is in danger. And I think yours is too."

One AM, closing time at the Dill Docks Club.

The poker game broke up and the members were escorted to their limousines, their liveried drivers standing around in the dark chewing tobacco, spitting, watching the fire flies illuminate the swamp lands, passing around a pint of Four Roses.

Captain Hoke made his rounds of the girls' rooms, chasing out one or two of the members who could never get enough. Then, for the first time ever, he checked on Dick.

Dick sat reading in his sitting room, dressed in boxers, smoking, enjoying a Jameson on ice. The door opened suddenly and Hoke stepped inside his cop eyes darting as if something might be hiding there. Dick didn't get up.

"Time for bed, Kid," Hoke grinned taking another step inside as if privileged.

Dick put down his drink. "You want something?"

"Just having a look."

"You had it. Get the fuck out."

"Dicky boy, we're starting to wonder about you. You better straighten out. I'm telling you for your own good."

"I'm not the marrying type. If that's a problem, Lemke can fire me. I'll go back to humpin' tie rods. Now get lost before I throw you out."

"Dick, don't ever get in the way of the flow of money. That's an unforgivable sin in this town."

Hoke backed out. Dick got up and watched the precinct commander in his starched white captain's shirt walk the long, dim hall, opening doors and getting called out by the girls. At the end of the hall he disappeared down the stairs. Dick waited a minute. All quiet. He pulled on dungarees and a T-shirt and went to January's room.

They left by way of the kitchen, took a path thru the weeds that was dry when the tide was out and climbed the embankment to where Dick had his car hidden in the willows. In a minute they were on 177th Street heading for Bruckner Boulevard and the distant glow of Manhattan where the Empire State Building jutted majestically toward the sky.

January's friend Trudie let them in, gave them both grey coveralls. The high speed elevators shot them up to the offices of Rosen Rahilley and Lemke Attorneys and Counselors at Law. Big gold block letters hung on the wall like picture frames. No one at the black marble reception desk. They found Lemke's office and searched around not finding anything except the safe.

They stood for a moment staring at the thick, black safe that could withstand a bomb blast.

"Let's have a look in the file cabinets," said January. She found a file on Flattop but there was nothing in it but general information, his legal name, address, business affairs. A secretary, not understanding much about security, had taped inside the file jacket a tiny manila envelope labelled: dead files, basement storage.

The tiny envelope contained a key with a number stamped on it.

They went downstairs and found Trudie. She examined the key and took them to a subbasement where there was a line of storage rooms, each one numbered. She found the correct door, turned the key and let them into a vault-like room with steel shelves containing storage cartons of dusty files. Trudie backed away, showing a little annoyance, complaining she could lose her job over this crap.

January smiled, touched her shoulder. "We won't be a minute. We'll leave the uniforms by the elevators and let ourselves out."

"My boss went out to eat an hour ago. He'll be back any minute. Don't let him catch you. He's a bastard. He'll have you arrested for breaking and entering."

Inside the room, the shelved cardboard storage boxes were labelled by year. January drifted slowly between the rows of shelves.

"What year did they put you in the Foundling Home?"

"I was ten, 1938."

She found a carton with that year stenciled on it and pulled it out. Dick grabbed the weighty box and set it on the floor. January dug into it like a terrier, her fingers nimble, rifling through the file folders.

She turned up a file labelled Foundling. Inside were newspaper clippings. Her eyes speed read the stories, not saying anything to Dick before she digested the content.

She read aloud, *"'Woman found cremated in remote section of the Bronx. Officers from the 45th Precinct found a funeral pyre and the burned remains of a young woman on a little used cinder road that passes through a series of marshes in the Throgs Neck section of the Bronx. A source stated the body appeared to have been butchered before it was burned. Police refused to confirm or deny. A search of the surrounding marshland found a ten year old boy hiding in the reeds. He was reported to be mute and frightened. His identity was not available. Cops reported he was sent to a hospital asylum in Kings Park, Long Island for observation…'"*

January asked Dick, "Could that boy be you?" She was still scanning the newsprint, not looking at Dick. When he made no reply, she turned toward him.

Dick had folded up on the floor.

"Dick, what's wrong?"

"Christ, oh fuckin' Christ," was all Dick could get out, saying it over and over, his hands clamped on his head as if it might explode.

She grabbed his shoulders, forcing him to look at her. "Pull yourself together."

"I'm trying. Jesus, it's like getting run over by a truck." His breath coming sharp and shallow. "I can almost see it. I can almost fuckin' see it."

"You remember?"

"I have dreams, nightmares. I've told you about them. But no memory. Unless you call feeling a memory. I can't remember it in any normal way. It's blurred in my mind. Something happened to the memory."

"But it is a memory, isn't it? This was something you experienced?"

"I think that's me, that boy in the news."

January perused the rest of the article. "They took you to Kings Park. You know what they do there?"

"I ... I don't know."

"I've known girls, crazy girls, who were sent there. They came out they didn't act crazy anymore. Just blank looks on their faces. They do electric shock there. They do lobotomies. They make bad memories go away."

"I don't remember being there. Except in dreams, like tunnel vision. A green walled institution. A dismal, lonely feeling. Something's twisted in my head. I can feel the memory, feel the fear, but I can't fuckin' see it. Only in dreams. It's like being haunted by a ghost.

"Do you want to stop?"

"No."

"There's a follow-up article. She read: *Police are looking for a man, possibly the boy's father.*

"Do they give a name?"

"No. No names."

She was lying. She didn't tell the name of the woman in the fire. The article read, - *determined by dental records as Nora Hennessey. She worked as a psychiatric nurse in Pilgrim State Hospital. It is believed she was murdered, although an accidental death has not been ruled out.*

"How about the woman in the fire? Do they name her?"

"No, I don't see anything," said January.

January thumbed through more papers and there it was, an old copy of Flattop's will. Superseded by a later copy but not destroyed. She was quiet for a moment, engrossed in reading

"What?" he asked.

"Nothing. Old documents."

She saw Dick's name, Richard Hennessey, listed as executor and Melissa Horan as sole heir. It didn't say Melissa was offspring of Flattop. But if she married Dick and then died, Dick would have right of survivorship and ownership of the real estate.

Dick's head rose and January quickly scanned the rest of the document. She didn't think Dick could handle that bit of information. What she didn't know is how the most recent copy of the will read. Is Dick still the executor? Would first-cousin marriage to Melissa be legal, if indeed that was Lemke's plan? She took another look at the final pages of the will. It stated, *Should there be no living heir the estate will be administered by the Lemke law firm.*

It appeared to January that Lemke would be much better off if Melissa and Dick were married – followed by Melissa's sudden death. Then what? Right of Survivorship. Dick would have control of the land and its sale price. But how would Lemke gain control, if that was his aim?

A sour scene with Lemke appeared in her mind, the man grabbing her, rushing her into Dick's private quarters, Dick not around, the man in a sexual rage, bending her over the back of the sofa, pulling her hair back like a leash. Did that mean anything? She wondered, *was he just violently fucking me? Or was it something more? A deliberate defilement. Of me? Or of Dick Hennessey? Or both of us?*

Dick was staring at her. She closed the flaps of the carton.

"Put the carton back on the shelf. Let's get out of here. I'm dying for a smoke, she said. She slipped the storage room key into her bra thinking she had to maneuver Dick. Get him on track. Do it right and she could take it all. Do it wrong and they'd both be dead.

XVII

FROM THE DUSTY MESA

DAVID BUSBOOM

When I was six I met a hoodoo man. This was in the summer of 1958; my family was on vacation in Mississippi and we were exploring Vicksburg. While my parents window-shopped I stalked around their legs and watched the people on the sidewalk. That's when I saw him at the end of the block.

He was an old black man in an antique wooden wheelchair, with wiry legs no thicker than my own six-year-old limbs, and hard-looking arms wide as my torso, I guess from rolling himself around everywhere. He was facing the street, watching the cars go by, I thought, but when I took a step toward him he turned his head and looked at me like he'd known I was there the whole time.

His scalp was covered in patches of thick, tight curls that were more black than grey, and his eyes smiled even though his mouth did not. One eye—the left—looked a little milky. The other was bright as glass.

I went over to him then, told him hello in my meek six-year-old voice. I said my name was Tommy and he said his name was Moses and I saw his big yellow teeth. He had a soft, deep voice. I said did he mean Moses like from the Bible and he said yessuh and I said I never read the Bible but my mommy and daddy talked about it. He pointed a bony claw at my parents and said was that my mommy and daddy and I said yes and he said his mommy and daddy were slaves before he was born. I said what were they after he was born and he said his daddy was a corpse and his mommy was a magic woman and I said what's a magic woman and he got real serious and said a vessel of The Masked Prophet.

"Anythin' you do is the plan of The Masked Prophet, understand," he explained, "The Pallid One. He have somethin' to do with everythin' you do, if it's good or bad, He have somethin' to do with it. Jis what's for you, you'll get it."

"That sounds like God," I said.

"He's a little like God, not quite as powerful, but a little more practical, maybe." He paused thoughtfully, searching for a way to explain. "Whenever I'm afraid of goin' to Hell I read the Bible and pray to God. Whenever I'm afraid of someone doin' me harm in this world I turn to The Masked Prophet. He came from way back yonder the time that the Bible's Moses lived, before the Bible was written or the church found. But you won't find Him in there."

"Why not?"

He looked into my eyes, his right eye sharp. "Not sure myself, but I 'spect it's 'cause the Bible says we was made in God's image. The Masked Prophet ain't that way. He says we more like fleas on a rat—but He still looks after us who know Him." He added this last as though trying to be comforting; whether to me or himself, I don't know.

"What does he look like?"

He frowned. "He's big and thin, with long white robes. Terrible to look on; never seen His face, though, on account of that mask."

After that my parents noticed where I was and with whom I was talking and they pulled me away, apologizing to the old cripple for letting their child bother him but really thinking it was Moses who'd bothered me. They marched me swiftly away, warned me never to approach strangers—especially strangers like *that*—and we finished our vacation and went home to Chicago without mentioning it again.

Over the years I forgot all about the hoodoo man and his strange words. I started reading true crime stories, smoking cigars, drinking whisky, chasing freckled girls and homicidal maniacs. I moved to Texas. I grew a moustache. I got married, shot at, divorced. I barely remembered that I'd ever even been to Mississippi.

Now, crouching in the South Texas desert outside Raptor Mesa, Beretta in hand and almost thirteen years eligible for retirement, I have Moses on my mind.

In quiet dusk, under the swollen moon, I am reborn. The Pallid One is in the wind, in the rocks, and I walk with Him among the blooming *Opuntia*. His eyes watch me from every direction, but they are not like the eyes of the old men at the hospital; no lust in His gaze, only pure love and warmth. I wonder if He will let me see Him tonight. He let me see Him once before, after the *adicto*, but He wouldn't unmask for me. He said I must do more if I want to see His face. I do.

Carmelita is meeting me out here tonight. She doesn't know He is with me.

The first body was found toward the end of May, not even three weeks ago. Naked, middle-aged Caucasian male, clothes scattered about in a twenty-foot radius, bones exposed in places where scavenging animals had torn away the flesh, eyes and genitals eaten away, flies and yellow maggots crawling in the wounds. Ugly and grim, but little I hadn't seen before in four decades of law enforcement. No obvious cause of death, but in the corpse's mouth was a playing card, the King of Clubs, on the back of which were two lines neatly typed:

> When the gibbous moon and black stars rise,
> The Pallid One has a thousand eyes.

For the first time in over fifty years I remembered Moses in Vicksburg. I ran the capitalized phrase through every search engine and database on the Internet, but found nothing useful—only brief, dated references as vague as the message on the card. Forensic analysis indicated that the note was typed on a Smith Corona manual typewriter, and yielded no usable fingerprints.

For kicks, I searched for records of men named

Moses living in Vicksburg during the late fifties and found only a bare-bones 1959 obituary for a Moses Wells, aged seventy-eight; a taxidermist, no family, never married. No photograph.

Expired driver's license in the corpse's discarded shorts identified it as Murray Browne, a local junkie who hadn't been seen for about two weeks and had probably only been missed by his dealer. Next of kin was a cousin two states away who claimed not to have spoken to Browne in almost fifteen years and wanted nothing to do with him now.

Autopsy revealed a small puncture wound in Browne's neck, and that the cause of death was a probable morphine overdose. It also revealed that, though all of the bite wounds were inflicted post-mortem, the oldest teeth marks appeared to be human.

A search of Browne's home—a rundown three-room trailer with dim furniture and lighting—yielded the typewriter: a pale blue model from the seventies. And next to the machine, a full deck of playing cards, minus the kings. There was a small radio and several books, but no television, computer, or phone—though there was no sign of a struggle and little indication that such items had ever been there. I doubted a robbery. There were also various pieces of drug paraphernalia (including syringes

and needles, but none that matched the puncture wound),
a small bag of heroin, a loaded Smith & Wesson .38
Special revolver, and scattered sheets of paper containing
mediocre poetry occasionally referring to a "Maria"
and, more often, a "Carmelita" (presumably written by
Browne), but no morphine and no further references
to "The Pallid One." Only prints in the place were
Browne's.

"Carmelita" was the popular moniker of Carmen
Jimenez, a stripper at The Dragon's Lair near the edge
of town. I'd seen her there more than a few times myself;
petite Latina in her early thirties, very pretty face, black
hair trimmed short like a little boy's and gelled into spikes
up front. The few locals who recalled seeing Browne
two weeks prior said he'd been at the Lair, so when I
went there to ask around I figured Jimenez was a good
place to start. She said he'd been there often in the past
few months, and that she was his favorite for lap dances,
when he could afford them. I asked her if they had any
relationship outside the Lair, and she said not to tell
anybody but she didn't swing that way if I knew what she
meant. I did.

"When was the last time you saw Mr. Browne?"

"Must be a little over two weeks ago. He came in
like normal, had a few drinks, bought a dance from me

and tried to flirt, *como siempre.* Poor Murray."

"Did he talk about anything unusual? Any special problems he was having? Strange people he'd met?"

"No, just flirted." She giggled sadly. "Joked about pawning his TV so he could keep seeing me."

"Anything else happen?"

"No, he left right after the dance."

"Was he alone?"

Jimenez nodded. "Yes. He was always solo."

"Okay. Do you know anyone named Maria? The name came up in some—uh—papers we found at Mr. Browne's home."

She looked surprised. "Only two: Maria Peraza and Maria Vasquez. Peraza works here, but I don't think Murray ever bought a dance from her. She didn't like him, anyway."

"Is she here tonight?"

"No, she's off tonight. But she'll be in tomorrow."

"What about Vasquez?"

"She's a nurse at Borderland. Took care of my mama last year before she passed, we became friends." She blushed. "Not very chatty, though. Think she got some issues herself."

"Did she know Mr. Browne?"

"No idea. Murray was a little crazy, I guess, but I

don't know if he was ever in the ward."

"All right, one last thing. Does the phrase, 'The Pallid One,' mean anything to you?"

She looked puzzled. "No, should it?"

Now it was my turn to shake my head. "No, probably not. Thanks for your time, Miss Jimenez."

She smiled, and it put lights in her green eyes. "*Carmelita. Ya lo sabes*, Tom."

I smiled back. "*No cuando es un asunto oficial*, I don't."

"*Muy bien*," she smirked. "*Detective Wilson*."

I made a circuit of the Lair, interviewed the other patrons and dancers present, but learned nothing new. I called the Borderlands House psych ward and learned that Browne had briefly checked himself in almost a year ago, stayed one week, and checked himself out. Couldn't tell me why, but said he'd been well-behaved and cooperative. When I asked to speak to Maria Vasquez the woman on the phone said she was out sick and was expected back in a day or two. Said Vasquez was quiet, but good with patients. Said there'd been a minor incident back in March with a couple of the lecherous older men in the ward, but it had been handled. She couldn't recall Vasquez having any contact with Browne during his stay.

I looked Vasquez up: another Latina about Jimenez's age, maybe a little older, and almost as pretty, with dark hair that hung past her shoulders; a U.S. citizen for nearly twenty years, no criminal record. I doubted her involvement or usefulness.

I returned to the Lair the following night and interviewed Peraza, a twenty-something with dark eyes and large breasts. She was disgusted at the mention of Browne, not surprised or upset by his passing, and tight-lipped. Said she was working during Browne's approximate time of death, which I confirmed with the manager on my way out. I looked her up and found a previous arrest for drug possession, when she was a teenager. Paid a fine, spent six months in jail, and had been working at the Lair since she turned eighteen. Born and raised in Raptor Mesa. I doubted her involvement, too, but she'd seen Browne on a fairly regular basis in the months before his murder, and her reticence made me suspicious. I decided to try and get a warrant to search her home. You never know what might prove useful in a case like this—or what weird things people are into.

The silver moon and the summer air help Him guide my hands. We are both naked, and I kill her like I did the *adicto*: a quick sting in the throat while we kiss. Her arms fall away from me and she stumbles backward, quivering and gasping shallowly like a fish. She looks at me before she loses balance and I see confusion in her face. I want to take it back, but He caresses me and breathes in my ear, and I know it is what He wants.

She lands on her side, on top of an *Opuntia* tangle, and rolls face-down in the sand; the cactus thorns stick in her skin, turning her into a mutant hybrid of some spiny creature. The gasping stops. I kneel over her and touch her trembling hand, wanting to cry but knowing He would not approve. Then she is still.

He appears, then, a pale shadow in the moonlight, and tells me to finish my work. I don't want to, but I know He'll never unmask for me otherwise. I must make Him happy. I must see His face.

Last night Carmen Jimenez never showed up for work. She was reported missing by a friend this morning. Nobody had seen or heard from her since night before last, and nobody knew where she'd gone.

I'm kneeling over her corpse now, less than half a mile from where Browne was found. In the boiling Texas sun the flies are imperturbable. She's naked, lying on her back, full of prickly pear spines on one side, small puncture wound in the other side of her neck, clothes in a loose pile just a few yards away. When I found her there were a few black vultures gathered around. I scared them off with a couple of shots from my Beretta, but they'd already taken the softest pieces of her.

There are bites missing from her torso and limbs, though, that aren't the vultures' work. Ragged crescents and ovals made by a smallish mouth, spaced far apart on her body. Such deliberate placement was not detectable on nearly-half-eaten Browne. I touch Carmelita's skin and my fingers come away bloody. There's a throbbing pressure in my head and a tightness in my chest and I think I may be sick, or cry, or both.

Delicately, gripping its edges with thumb and blood-tipped forefinger, I pull the playing card from between her teeth: the King of Hearts. On the back another typed couplet:

> Though songs are sung and tears are shed,
> The Pallid One is never dead.

"Goddamn it," I sigh.

The blood is pounding in my ears. I'm thinking of Moses when a shadow falls over me. Before I can turn the pain comes, sharp and quick, in my back. It's gone as quickly as it arrives and now I feel tired and much too warm on this already hot day. I pitch forward and heave myself to one side to avoid landing on Jimenez. I'm nauseous and dizzy, on my back in the blood-speckled sand. I can barely hold my head up, can barely breathe. My head is pounding. Maria Vasquez stands over me, wearing frayed jeans and a stained John Lennon T-shirt, syringe held up in one latex-gloved hand. Behind her a tall, thin figure looms, nearly twice as high as the man-sized creosote bushes. It wears tattered pale robes that flap in the breeze, almost yellow with age and dirt. Its face is covered by a featureless bone-white mask, ovoid and smooth. I try to lift the Beretta but it's so heavy and my hands are trembling. I just want to go to sleep.

After I've done my work I wipe the blood from my lips and take one of the last two cards from my pocket: the King of Spades.

But death is not the end, rejoice!
The Pallid One has made His choice.

I place the card in the detective's mouth. The Pallid One stands beside me and whispers His approval. I want to ask Him how He knew the detective would be here, how He knew he'd be alone, how He knew I would succeed—but to ask such questions would only annoy Him, I'm sure. He says He will unmask for me now, if I'll just follow his last instructions. Of course I will. He tells me to take off my clothes. I do. He tells me to take the last card, the King of Diamonds. This one has nothing typed on it. He tells me to put it in my mouth. I do as He tells me and stand facing Him, staring up into that shining oval. My tears are no longer sad. I regret nothing. I am not afraid. I have earned my reward.

He lifts a pair of slender, ashen hands and—carefully, tenderly—removes His mask.

XVIII

THE DARK SIDE

Andrew
Shaffer

"People out here, it's like they don't even know the outside world exists. Might as well be living on the fucking moon."
- Rust Cohle

The beep jolted Nick Ligotti awake. "We're preparing for descent," a voice said over the intercom. It was the deep baritone of an older man. "We'll be on the lunar surface in approximately ten minutes. The temperature is…well, it doesn't matter what the temperature is, does it?"

The recording got a few light laughs from the rubes in economy. Ligotti had heard variations of this joke dozens of times. He'd almost smirked the first time he'd heard it. Almost.

Malaysian was one of the few airlines that even bothered to give the impression their flights were piloted by actual human beings. Apparently, it soothed the nerves of the elderly passengers. Ligotti put more faith in the ship's guidance systems and ground control than in flesh-and-blood pilots. Computers didn't down a few beers before flying; computers didn't get distracted by cheating spouses. People were inherently flawed creations. God may have made humanity in His image, but Charles Babbage one-upped Him.

"You were snoring."

Ligotti glanced at the aisle seat beside him. It had been empty when he'd dozed off. A boy of eight or so was sitting on his knees, staring at Ligotti as if he were a zoo exhibit. Fitting, since Ligotti's only distinct memory of the zoo he visited as a kid was the napping *Triceratops*. So wild, so majestic...so lazy.

A sharply-dressed male flight attendant walked down the aisle, giving each passenger's lap a cursory glance. The airlines hadn't figured out a way to dispense with flight attendants yet, because people couldn't be trusted to buckle their seatbelts. People. Flawed creations.

"Face forward and buckle up," the flight attendant told the boy.

The boy sat down and buckled the seatbelt.

"If you snore, it might be a sign of sleep apnoea," the boy said to Ligotti. "My dad had sleep apnoea. He had to be hooked up to a machine every night—"

"No offense to your dad, but I don't need a machine to breathe." Ligotti pulled the *SpaceMall* catalog out of the seatback pocket and thumbed through it.

"You should see a doctor."

"I'm not going to see a doctor, because I don't have sleep apnoea," Ligotti said without looking up from the magazine. "Okay?"

"Okay," the boy said. "If you stop breathing during the night—"

"I'd rather die peacefully in my sleep like my grandpa, and not screaming like the passengers in his LRV."

"Your grandpa died in his sleep? Even more reason to see a doctor. Sleep apnoea can be hereditary. That means—"

"I know what 'hereditary' means," Ligotti said.

Weren't this boy's parents worried that their son was out of his seat? Ligotti flipped the pages absentmindedly, and stopped on a page of lawn gnomes and assorted other outdoor ornaments.

The boy carefully studied him, then whispered, "You're a fed."

"Why do you say that?"

"The black suit and tie."

Ligotti sighed. The rest of the passengers,

including most of those in business class, were dressed in more casual threads. Feds didn't have a uniform *per se*, but they were required to adhere to a strict dress code when on the clock. Ligotti was salaried, so he was pretty much always on the clock.

"I'm a property assessor," he explained. "A tax man."

"Sounds boring."

"Work is boring. That's why it's called work." Ligotti shoved the catalog back into the pocket. He just wanted to land, take the shuttle to his hotel, fap to some adult entertainment, and fall back asleep. He'd taken enough barbies to knock out a man twice his size for a week. They were beginning to pull him back under. His eyelids felt like lead blankets....

"My mom says if you love your job, you'll never work a day in your life."

Ligotti snorted. "Is that so?"

"I'm going to be an artist. I like to draw. That way, I'll never have to work."

"That's because you'll be unemployed," Ligotti quipped.

"My dad was unemployed."

"Then what happened? He get a job?"

The boy paused. "He died," he said quietly.

"I'm sorry," Ligotti said.

"It's okay," the boy said, perking back up. "I don't really remember him—except for his sleep machine. Mama says he was a real prick."

The boy's frank manner when speaking about his deceased father might have shocked another passenger, but Ligotti was unfazed. He glanced around the cabin, looking for the boy's empty seat. "You traveling with your mom?"

The boy fidgeted with the TV controls on the seatback. "She's on Miranda."

"Traveling alone?"

"I've flown alone lots."

Ligotti nodded. "So what's on the Moon?"

"Grandma."

"Whereabouts?"

"Huntington."

The Far Side of the Moon. In less polite conversation, the largely impoverished area was referred to by its original nickname: the Dark Side. Not that it was lacking in illumination—both the Near Side and Far Side receive roughly the same amount of sunlight. No, the difference wasn't sunlight. The difference was darkness of another sort.

"You don't sound like you're from the Far Side," Ligotti said.

"Soon as my dad died, Mama moved us to Miranda," the boy said. "She said she didn't want to raise no moony." For this last bit, the boy affected a twang.

Ligotti laughed, though he probably shouldn't have. Wasn't much funny about moonies. His gaze drifted out the window. They were passing over the featureless dunes on the Far Side—barely lit up at the moment, in the days-long twilight.

The closer they cruised to the surface, the more settlements he could pick out amongst the fine grey sand. This wasn't, to say the least, prime real estate. The near side, with its breathtaking views of the Earth, was far more populated. Out here, though…well, "harsh" wasn't a harsh enough word to describe the living conditions. And he was going to spend the next eighteen months knocking on airlocks and poking his nose around this dirt hellhole.

As the ground drew closer and closer, Ligotti closed his eyes and silently prayed for an accident. A glitch buried deep within in the ship's software, revealing itself at the moment before touchdown, resulting in a terrific crash into the runway—an inferno, quickly extinguished by the Moon's lack of oxygen. Before it went out, the fire would burn through every body on board, delivering them from this godforsaken rock in a matter of seconds. Was it suicide to pray for your own death?

The ship touched down smoothly on the runway and slowed to a stop. He heard the other passengers unbuckling. How many of them had been praying for an accident as well? Ligotti opened his eyes and looked around. A quarter of them? A benevolent creator would have answered their collective prayer and put them out of their misery—all of them, including the boy. A benevolent creator would have spared the boy the sin of growing old. A benevolent creator wouldn't let his crops grow up and wilt on the vine.

The boy was right about one thing. Heredity is an unforgiving bitch. Genetics guaran-damn-teed that. The boy was smart, but the Dark Side was baked into his soul. Ligotti could see the darkness in his eyes; he could sense it when the boy spoke about his father. He may have shed his dear ol' dad's accent, but it was safe to say he wouldn't be splitting the atom. The Dark Side had a funny way of following you around, no matter what rock you escaped to.

Ligotti knew this because the darkness was in his own DNA.

It had taken him years to scrub all traces of the twang from his voice. He thought he'd escaped the Dark Side long ago. But here he was, returning to his lunar roots like a salmon swimming upstream to spawn. To spawn and die. Was that free will? He didn't know. He'd taken the only transfer available. He hadn't been worried where he was going, just that he was leaving Europa. Everything in his home reminded him—no, *taunted* him—of his loss. It wasn't enough just into move to a new apartment, either. Even the brilliant blood-orange sunsets reminded him that his wife was gone. No matter how much dirt he shoveled into that particular grave, it was an open wound. The only way to deal with that type of pain was to walk away. Forget about it.

"You okay?" the boy asked, snapping Ligotti out of his thoughts.

"Okay?" he said. "I haven't been okay for a long time."

Confusion spread on the boy's face. "I meant that you look like you're going to be sick."

"Then you'd better get back to your own seat, before I get sick on you."

The boy quickly unbuckled his seatbelt. He shot one last worried look at Ligotti, who put a hand to his mouth as if he were on the verge of throwing up. The boy disappeared down the crowded aisle, passing through the passengers stretching their legs and removing bags from the overhead bins.

"Welcome to the Moon, where the local time is eleven thirty-eight," the recorded voice said over the intercom. "And if this is your final destination, welcome home."

www.ingramcontent.com/pod-product-compliance
Lightning Source LLC
Chambersburg PA
CBHW070917190726
48292CB00004B/1008